JAMAICA KINCAID was born in St. John's, Antigua, in the
West Indies. She is a staff writer for *The New Yorker;* her stories
have also appeared in *Rolling Stone* and *The Paris Review.* Her pre-
vious book, *At the Bottom of the River*, won the Morton Dauwen
Zabel Award of the American Academy and Institute of Arts and
Letters.

P9-CAB-196

Annie John

Jamaica Kincaid

A PLUME BOOK

PLUME
Published by the Penguin Group
Penguin Books USA Inc., 375 Hudson Street, New York, New York 10014,
U.S.A.
Penguin Books Ltd, 27 Wrights Lane, London W8 5TZ, England
Penguin Books Australia Ltd, Ringwood, Victoria, Australia
Penguin Books Canada Ltd, 2801 John Street, Markham, Ontario, Canada
L3R 1B4
Penguin Books (N.Z.) Ltd, 182-190 Wairau Road, Auckland 10, New Zealand

Penguin Books Ltd, Registered Offices: Harmondsworth, Middlesex, England

Published by Plume, an imprint of New American Library, a division of
Penguin Books USA Inc.

This is an authorized reprint of a hardcover edition published by Farrar, Straus
& Giroux, Inc., and simultaneously in Canada by Collins Publishers, Toronto.

Acknowledgment is made to *The New Yorker*, where the text of this book first
appeared, in slightly different form.

REG. TRADEMARK—MARCA REGISTRADA

Library of Congress Cataloging-in-Publication Data
Kincaid, Jamaica.
    Annie John.
    i. Title.
[PS3561.I425A55   1986]   813'.54   85-29760
ISBN 0-452-26356-5 (pbk.)

First Plume Printing, May, 1986

8   9   10   11   12   13   14   15   16

PRINTED IN THE UNITED STATES OF AMERICA

For Allen, with love

Contents

Annie John

Chapter One

Figures in the Distance

For a short while during the year I was ten, I thought only people I did not know died. At the time I thought this I was on my summer holidays and we were living far out on Fort Road. Usually, we lived in our house on Dickenson Bay Street, a house my father built with his own hands, but just now it needed a new roof and so we were living in a house out on Fort Road. We had only two neighbors, Mistress Maynard and her husband. That summer, we had a pig that had just had piglets; some guinea fowl; and some ducks that laid enormous eggs that my mother said were big even for ducks. I hated to eat any food except for the enormous duck eggs, hard-boiled. I had nothing to do every day except to feed the birds and the pig in the morning and in the evening. I spoke to no one other than my parents, and sometimes to Mistress Maynard, if I saw her when I went to pick up the peelings of vegetables which my mother had asked her to save for the pig, which was just the thing the pig really liked. From our yard, I could see the cemetery. I did not know it was the cemetery until one day when I said to my mother that sometimes in the evening, while feeding the pig, I could see various small, sticklike figures, some dressed in black, some dressed in white, bobbing up and down in the distance. I noticed, too, that sometimes the black and white sticklike figures appeared in the morning. My mother said that it was probably a child being buried, since children were always buried in the morning. Until then, I had not known that children died.

I was afraid of the dead, as was everyone I knew. We were afraid of the dead because we never could tell when they might show up again. Sometimes they showed up in a dream, but that wasn't so bad, because they usually only brought a warning, and in any case you wake up from a dream. But sometimes they would show up standing under a tree just as you were passing by. Then they might follow you home, and even though they might not be able to come into your house, they might wait for you and follow you wherever you went; in that case, they would never give up until you joined them. My mother knew of many people who had died in such a way. My mother knew of many people who had died, including her own brother.

After I found out about the cemetery, I would stand in my yard and wait for a funeral to come.

Some days, there were no funerals. "No one died," I would say to my mother. Some days, just as I was about to give up and go inside, I would see the small specks appear. "What made them so late?" I would ask my mother. Probably someone couldn't bear to see the coffin lid put in place, and so as a favor the undertaker might let things go on too long, she said. The undertaker! On our way into town, we would pass the undertaker's workshop. Outside, a little sign read "STRAFFEE & SONS, UNDERTAKERS & CABINET-MAKERS." I could always tell we were approaching this place, because of the smell of pitch pine and varnish in the air.

Later, we moved back to our house in town, and I no longer had a view of the cemetery. Still no one I knew had died. One day, a girl smaller than I, a girl whose mother was a friend of my mother's, died in my mother's arms. I did not know this girl at all, though I may have got a glimpse of her once or twice as I passed her and her mother coming out of our yard, and I tried to remember everything I had heard about her. Her name was Nalda; she had red hair; she was very bony; she did not like to eat any food. In fact, she liked to eat mud, and her mother always had to keep a strict eye on her to prevent her from doing that. Her father made bricks, and her mother dressed in a way that my father found unbecoming. I heard my mother describe to my father just how Nalda had died: She had a fever, they noticed a change in her breathing, so they called a car and were rushing her off to Dr. Bailey when, just as they were crossing over a bridge, she let out a long sigh and went limp. Dr. Bailey pronounced her dead, and when I heard that I was so glad he wasn't my doctor. My mother asked my father to make the coffin for Nalda, and he did, carving bunches of tiny flowers on the sides. Nalda's mother wept so much that my mother had to take care of everything, and since children were never prepared by undertakers, my mother had to prepare the little girl to be buried. I then began to look at my mother's hands differently. They had stroked the dead girl's forehead; they had bathed and dressed her and laid her in the coffin my father had made. My mother would come back from the dead girl's house smelling of bay rum—a scent that for a long time afterward would make me feel ill. For a while, though not for very long, I could not bear to have my mother caress me or touch my food or help me with my bath. I especially couldn't bear the sight of her hands lying still in her lap.

At school, I told all my friends about this death. I would take them aside individually, so I could repeat the details over and over again. They would listen to me with their mouths open. In turn, they would tell me of someone they had known or heard of who had died. I would listen with my mouth open. One person had known very well a neighbor who had gone swimming after eating a big lunch at a picnic and drowned. Someone had a cousin who in the middle of something one day just fell down dead. Someone knew a boy who had died after eating some poisonous berries. "Fancy that," we said to each other.

I loved very much—and so used to torment until she cried—a girl named Sonia. She was smaller than I, even though she was almost two years older, and she was a dunce—the first real dunce I had ever met. She was such a dunce that sometimes she could not remember the spelling of her own name. I would try to get to school early and give her my homework, so that she could copy it, and in class I would pass her the answers to sums. My friends ignored her, and whenever I mentioned her name in a favorable way they would twist up their lips and make a sound to show their disdain. I thought her beautiful and I would say so. She had long, thick black hair that lay down flat on her arms and legs; and then running down the nape of her neck, down the middle of her back for as far as could be seen before it was swallowed up by her school uniform, was a line of the same long, thick black hair, only here it flared out as if a small breeze had come and parted it. At recess, I would buy her a sweet—something called a frozen joy—with money I had stolen from my mother's purse, and then we would go and sit under a tree in our schoolyard. I would then stare and stare at her, narrowing and opening wide my eyes until she began to fidget under my gaze. Then I would pull at the hair on her arms and legs—gently at first, and then awfully hard, holding it up taut with the tips of my fingers until she cried out. For a few weeks, she didn't appear in school, and we were told that her mother, who had been with child, had died suddenly. I couldn't ever again bring myself to speak to her, even though we spent two more years as classmates. She seemed such a shameful thing, a girl whose mother had died and left her alone in the world.

Not long after the little girl died in my mother's arms on the way to the doctor, Miss Charlotte, our neighbor across the street, collapsed and died while having a conversation with my mother. If my mother hadn't caught her, she would have fallen to the ground. When I came home from school that day, my mother said, "Miss Charlotte is dead." I had known Miss Charlotte very well, and I tried to imagine her dead. I couldn't. I did not know what someone looked like dead. I knew what Miss Charlotte looked like coming from market. I knew what she looked like going to church. I knew what she looked like when she told her dog not to frighten me by chasing me up and down the street. Once, when Miss Charlotte was sick, my mother asked me to take her a bowl with some food, so I saw her lying in her bed in her nightgown. Miss Charlotte was buried in a coffin my father did not make, and I was not allowed to go to the funeral.

At school, almost everyone I knew had seen a dead person, and not a spirit of a dead person but a real dead person. The girl who sat at the desk next to mine suddenly stopped sucking her thumb because her mother had washed it in water in which a dead person had been given a bath. I told her that her mother must have been playing a trick on her, that I was sure the water was plain water, since it was just the sort of trick my mother would play on me. But she had met my mother and she said she could see that my mother and her mother weren't alike at all.

I began to go to funerals. I didn't actually go to the funerals as an official mourner, since I didn't know any of the people who had died and I was going without my parents' permission. I visited the funeral parlors or the drawing rooms where the dead were laid out for viewing by the mourners. When I heard the church bell toll in the way it tolled when someone had died, I would try to find out who had died and where the funeral was to be—home or funeral parlor. The funeral parlor was in much the same direction as my route home, but sometimes to get to someone's house I would have to go in the opposite direction of my way home. At first, I didn't go in; I would just stand outside and watch the people come and go, hear the close relatives and friends let out incredible loud wails and moans, and then watch the procession march off to church. But then I began to go in and take a look. The first time I actually saw a dead person, I didn't know what to think. Since it wasn't someone I knew, I couldn't make a comparison. I had never seen the person laugh or smile or frown or shoo a chicken out of a garden. So I looked and looked for as long as I could without letting anyone know I was just there out of curiosity.

One day, a girl my own age died. I did not know

her name or anything personal about her except that she was my own age and that she had a humpback. She attended another school, and on the day of her funeral her whole school got the day off. At my school, it was all we could talk about: "Did you know the humpbacked girl?" I remembered once standing behind her in a line to take out books at the library; then I saw a fly land on the collar of her uniform and walk up and down as the collar lay flat on her hump. On hearing that she was dead, I wished I had tapped the hump to see if it was hollow. I also remembered that her hair was parted into four plaits and that the parts were crooked. "She must have combed her hair herself," I said. At last, though, someone I knew was dead. The day of her funeral, I bolted from school as soon as we finished the last amen of our evening prayers, and I made my way to the funeral home. When I got there, the whole street was full of girls from her school, all in their white dress uniforms. It was a big crowd of them, and they were milling around, talking to each other quietly and looking very important. I didn't have time to stop and really envy them; I made my way to the door and entered the funeral parlor. There she was. She was lying in the regular pitch-pine, varnished coffin, on a bed of mauve-and-white lilacs. She wore a white dress, and it may have come all the way down to her ankles, but I didn't have time to look carefully. It was her face that I wanted to see. I remembered how she had looked the day in the library. Her face was just a plain face. She had black eyes, flat nostrils, broad lips. Lying there dead, she looked the same, except her eyes were closed and she was so still. I once had heard someone say about another dead person that it was as if the dead person were asleep. But I had seen a person asleep, and this girl did not look asleep. My parents had just bought me a View-Master. The View-Master came with pictures of the pyramids, the Taj Mahal, Mt. Everest, and scenes of the Amazon River. When the View-Master worked properly, all the scenes looked as if they were alive, as if we could just step into the View-Master and sail down the Amazon River or stand at the foot of the pyramids. When the View-Master didn't work properly, it was as if we were looking at an ordinary, colorful picture. When I looked at this girl, it was as if the View-Master wasn't working properly. I stared at her a long time—long enough so that I caused the line of people waiting to stop by the coffin to grow long and on the verge of impatience. Of course, as I stared I kept my fingers curled up tight against my palms, because I didn't want to make a mistake and point and then have them rot and drop off right there. I then went and sat among the mourners. Her family smiled at me, thinking, I am sure, that I was a school friend, even though I wore the uniform of another school. We sang a hymn—"All Things Bright and Beautiful"—and her mother said it was the first hymn the humpbacked girl had learned to sing by heart.

I walked home. By then, I was very late getting home from school, but I was too excited to worry about it. I wondered if one day while going some-

where alone I would see the humpbacked girl standing under a tree, and if she would try to get me to go
for a swim or eat a piece of fruit, and the next thing
my mother would know, she would be asking my
father to make a coffin for me. Of course, he would
be so overcome with grief he wouldn't be able to
make my coffin and would have to ask Mr. Oatie to
do it, and he just hated to ask Mr. Oatie to do him a
favor, because, as I heard him tell my mother, Mr.
Oatie was such a leech he tried to suck you dry by
making you pay for everything twice.

When I got home, my mother asked me for the
fish I was to have picked up from Mr. Earl, one of
our fishermen, on the way home from school. But in
my excitement I had completely forgotten. Trying to
think quickly, I said that when I got to the market
Mr. Earl told me that they hadn't gone to sea that
day because the sea was too rough. "Oh?" said my
mother, and uncovered a pan in which were lying,
flat on their sides and covered with lemon juice and
butter and onions, three fish: an angelfish for my
father, a kanya fish for my mother, and a lady doctorfish
for me—the special kind of fish each of us liked. While
I was at the funeral parlor, Mr. Earl had got tired of
waiting for me and had brought the fish to our house
himself. That night, as a punishment, I ate my supper
outside, alone, under the breadfruit tree, and my
mother said that she would not be kissing me good
night later, but when I climbed into bed she came
and kissed me anyway.

Chapter Two

The Circling Hand

During my holidays from school, I was allowed
to stay in bed until long after my father had gone
to work. He left our house every weekday at the
stroke of seven by the Anglican church bell. I would
lie in bed awake, and I could hear all the sounds my
parents made as they prepared for the day ahead. As
my mother made my father his breakfast, my father
would shave, using his shaving brush that had an
ivory handle and a razor that matched; then he would
step outside to the little shed he had built for us as a
bathroom, to quickly bathe in water that he had
instructed my mother to leave outside overnight in
the dew. That way, the water would be very cold, and
he believed that cold water strengthened his back. If
I had been a boy, I would have gotten the same treat-
ment, but since I was a girl, and on top of that went
to school only with other girls, my mother would

always add some hot water to my bathwater to take off the chill. On Sunday afternoons, while I was in Sunday school, my father took a hot bath; the tub was half filled with plain water, and then my mother would add a large caldronful of water in which she had just boiled some bark and leaves from a bay-leaf tree. The bark and leaves were there for no reason other than that he liked the smell. He would then spend hours lying in this bath, studying his pool coupons or drawing examples of pieces of furniture he planned to make. When I came home from Sunday school, we would sit down to our Sunday dinner.

My mother and I often took a bath together. Sometimes it was just a plain bath, which didn't take very long. Other times, it was a special bath in which the barks and flowers of many different trees, together with all sorts of oils, were boiled in the same large caldron. We would then sit in this bath in a darkened room with a strange-smelling candle burning away. As we sat in this bath, my mother would bathe different parts of my body; then she would do the same to herself. We took these baths after my mother had consulted with her obeah woman, and with her mother and a trusted friend, and all three of them had confirmed that from the look of things around our house—the way a small scratch on my instep had turned into a small sore, then a large sore, and how long it had taken to heal; the way a dog she knew, and a friendly dog at that, suddenly turned and bit her; how a porcelain bowl she had carried from one eternity and hoped to carry into the next suddenly slipped out of her capable hands and broke into pieces the size of grains of sand; how words she spoke in jest to a friend had been completely misunderstood—one of the many women my father had loved, had never married, but with whom he had had children was trying to harm my mother and me by setting bad spirits on us.

When I got up, I placed my bedclothes and my nightie in the sun to air out, brushed my teeth, and washed and dressed myself. My mother would then give me my breakfast, but since, during my holidays, I was not going to school, I wasn't forced to eat an enormous breakfast of porridge, eggs, an orange or half a grapefruit, bread and butter, and cheese. I could get away with just some bread and butter and cheese and porridge and cocoa. I spent the day following my mother around and observing the way she did everything. When we went to the grocer's, she would point out to me the reason she bought each thing. I was shown a loaf of bread or a pound of butter from at least ten different angles. When we went to market, if that day she wanted to buy some crabs she would inquire from the person selling them if they came from near Parham, and if the person said yes my mother did not buy the crabs. In Parham was the leper colony, and my mother was convinced that the crabs ate nothing but the food from the lepers' own plates. If we were then to eat the crabs, it wouldn't be long before we were lepers ourselves and living unhappily in the leper colony.

How important I felt to be with my mother. For

many people, their wares and provisions laid out in front of them, would brighten up when they saw her coming and would try hard to get her attention. They would dive underneath their stalls and bring out goods even better than what they had on display. They were disappointed when she held something up in the air, looked at it, turning it this way and that, and then, screwing up her face, said, "I don't think so," and turned and walked away—off to another stall to see if someone who only last week had sold her some delicious christophine had something that was just as good. They would call out after her turned back that next week they expected to have eddoes or dasheen or whatever, and my mother would say, "We'll see," in a very disbelieving tone of voice. If then we went to Mr. Kenneth, it would be only for a few minutes, for he knew exactly what my mother wanted and always had it ready for her. Mr. Kenneth had known me since I was a small child, and he would always remind me of little things I had done then as he fed me a piece of raw liver he had set aside for me. It was one of the few things I liked to eat, and, to boot, it pleased my mother to see me eat something that was so good for me, and she would tell me in great detail the effect the raw liver would have on my red blood corpuscles.

We walked home in the hot midmorning sun mostly without event. When I was much smaller, quite a few times while I was walking with my mother she would suddenly grab me and wrap me up in her skirt and drag me along with her as if in a great hurry.

I would hear an angry voice saying angry things, and
then, after we had passed the angry voice, my mother
would release me. Neither my mother nor my father
ever came straight out and told me anything, but I
had put two and two together and I knew that it was
one of the women that my father had loved and with
whom he had had a child or children, and who never
forgave him for marrying my mother and having me.
It was one of those women who were always trying to
harm my mother and me, and they must have loved
my father very much, for not once did any of them
ever try to hurt him, and whenever he passed them
on the street it was as if he and these women had
never met.

When we got home, my mother started to prepare
our lunch (pumpkin soup with droppers, banana
fritters with salt fish stewed in antroba and tomatoes,
fungie with salt fish stewed in antroba and tomatoes,
or pepper pot, all depending on what my mother had
found at market that day). As my mother went about
from pot to pot, stirring one, adding something to
the other, I was ever in her wake. As she dipped into
a pot of boiling something or other to taste for correct seasoning, she would give me a taste of it also,
asking me what I thought. Not that she really wanted
to know what I thought, for she had told me many
times that my taste buds were not quite developed
yet, but it was just to include me in everything. While
she made our lunch, she would also keep an eye on
her washing. If it was a Tuesday and the colored
clothes had been starched, as she placed them on the

line I would follow, carrying a basket of clothespins for her. While the starched colored clothes were being dried on the line, the white clothes were being whitened on the stone heap. It was a beautiful stone heap that my father had made for her: an enormous circle of stones, about six inches high, in the middle of our yard. On it the soapy white clothes were spread out; as the sun dried them, bleaching out all stains, they had to be made wet again by dousing them with buckets of water. On my holidays, I did this for my mother. As I watered the clothes, she would come up behind me, instructing me to get the clothes thoroughly wet, showing me a shirt that I should turn over so that the sleeves were exposed.

Over our lunch, my mother and father talked to each other about the houses my father had to build; how disgusted he had become with one of his apprentices, or with Mr. Oatie; what they thought of my schooling so far; what they thought of the noises Mr. Jarvis and his friends made for so many days when they locked themselves up inside Mr. Jarvis's house and drank rum and ate fish they had caught themselves and danced to the music of an accordion that they took turns playing. On and on they talked. As they talked, my head would move from side to side, looking at them. When my eyes rested on my father, I didn't think very much of the way he looked. But when my eyes rested on my mother, I found her beautiful. Her head looked as if it should be on a sixpence. What a beautiful long neck, and long plaited hair, which she pinned up around the crown

of her head because when her hair hung down it
made her too hot. Her nose was the shape of a flower
on the brink of opening. Her mouth, moving up and
down as she ate and talked at the same time, was such
a beautiful mouth I could have looked at it forever
if I had to and not mind. Her lips were wide and
almost thin, and when she said certain words I could
see small parts of big white teeth—so big, and pearly,
like some nice buttons on one of my dresses. I didn't
much care about what she said when she was in this
mood with my father. She made him laugh so. She
could hardly say a word before he would burst out
laughing. We ate our food, I cleared the table, we said
goodbye to my father as he went back to work, I helped
my mother with the dishes, and then we settled into
the afternoon.

When my mother, at sixteen, after quarreling
with her father, left his house on Dominica and came
to Antigua, she packed all her things in an enormous
wooden trunk that she had bought in Roseau for
almost six shillings. She painted the trunk yellow
and green outside, and she lined the inside with wall-
paper that had a cream background with pink roses
printed all over it. Two days after she left her father's
house, she boarded a boat and sailed for Antigua. It
was a small boat, and the trip would have taken a
day and a half ordinarily, but a hurricane blew up
and the boat was lost at sea for almost five days. By
the time it got to Antigua, the boat was practically
in splinters, and though two or three of the pas-

sengers were lost overboard, along with some of the cargo, my mother and her trunk were safe. Now, twenty-four years later, this trunk was kept under my bed, and in it were things that had belonged to me, starting from just before I was born. There was the chemise, made of white cotton, with scallop edging around the sleeves, neck, and hem, and white flowers embroidered on the front—the first garment I wore after being born. My mother had made that herself, and once, when we were passing by, I was even shown the tree under which she sat as she made this garment. There were some of my diapers, with their handkerchief hemstitch that she had also done herself; there was a pair of white wool booties with matching jacket and hat; there was a blanket in white wool and a blanket in white flannel cotton; there was a plain white linen hat with lace trimming; there was my christening outfit; there were two of my baby bottles: one in the shape of a normal baby bottle, and the other shaped like a boat, with a nipple on either end; there was a thermos in which my mother had kept a tea that was supposed to have a soothing effect on me; there was the dress I wore on my first birthday: a yellow cotton with green smocking on the front; there was the dress I wore on my second birthday: pink cotton with green smocking on the front; there was also a photograph of me on my second birthday wearing my pink dress and my first pair of earrings, a chain around my neck, and a pair of bracelets, all specially made of gold from British Guiana; there was the first pair of shoes

I grew out of after I knew how to walk; there was
the dress I wore when I first went to school, and the
first notebook in which I wrote; there were the sheets
for my crib and the sheets for my first bed; there was
my first straw hat, my first straw basket—decorated
with flowers—my grandmother had sent me from
Dominica; there were my report cards, my certificates
of merit from school, and my certificates of merit
from Sunday school.

From time to time, my mother would fix on a
certain place in our house and give it a good clean-
ing. If I was at home when she happened to do this,
I was at her side, as usual. When she did this with the
trunk, it was a tremendous pleasure, for after she had
removed all the things from the trunk, and aired
them out, and changed the camphor balls, and then
refolded the things and put them back in their places
in the trunk, as she held each thing in her hand she
would tell me a story about myself. Sometimes I knew
the story first hand, for I could remember the incident quite well; sometimes what she told me had
happened when I was too young to know anything;
and sometimes it happened before I was even born.
Whichever way, I knew exactly what she would say,
for I had heard it so many times before, but I never
got tired of it. For instance, the flowers on the
chemise, the first garment I wore after being born,
were not put on correctly, and that is because when
my mother was embroidering them I kicked so much
that her hand was unsteady. My mother said that
usually when I kicked around in her stomach and

she told me to stop I would, but on that day I paid no attention at all. When she told me this story, she would smile at me and say, "You see, even then you were hard to manage." It pleased me to think that, before she could see my face, my mother spoke to me in the same way she did now. On and on my mother would go. No small part of my life was so unimportant that she hadn't made a note of it, and now she would tell it to me over and over again. I would sit next to her and she would show me the very dress I wore on the day I bit another child my age with whom I was playing. "Your biting phase," she called it. Or the day she warned me not to play around the coal pot, because I liked to sing to myself and dance around the fire. Two seconds later, I fell into the hot coals, burning my elbows. My mother cried when she saw that it wasn't serious, and now, as she told me about it, she would kiss the little black patches of scars on my elbows.

As she told me the stories, I sometimes sat at her side, leaning against her, or I would crouch on my knees behind her back and lean over her shoulder. As I did this, I would occasionally sniff at her neck, or behind her ears, or at her hair. She smelled sometimes of lemons, sometimes of sage, sometimes of roses, sometimes of bay leaf. At times I would no longer hear what it was she was saying; I just liked to look at her mouth as it opened and closed over words, or as she laughed. How terrible it must be for all the people who had no one to love them so and no one whom they loved so, I thought. My father, for instance. When he was a little boy, his parents, after kissing him goodbye and leaving him with his grandmother, boarded a boat and sailed to South America. He never saw them again, though they wrote to him and sent him presents—packages of clothes on his birthday and at Christmas. He then grew to love his grandmother, and she loved him, for she took care of him and worked hard at keeping him well fed and clothed. From the beginning, they slept in the same bed, and as he became a young man they continued to do so. When he was no longer in school and had started working, every night, after he and his grandmother had eaten their dinner, my father would go off to visit his friends. He would then return home at around midnight and fall asleep next to his grandmother. In the morning, his grandmother would awake at half past five or so, a half hour before my father, and prepare his bath and breakfast and make everything proper and ready for him, so that at seven o'clock sharp he stepped out the door off to work. One morning, though, he overslept, because his grandmother didn't wake him up. When he awoke, she was still lying next to him. When he tried to wake her, he couldn't. She had died lying next to him sometime during the night. Even though he was overcome with grief, he built her coffin and made sure she had a nice funeral. He never slept in that bed again, and shortly afterward he moved out of that house. He was eighteen years old then.

When my father first told me this story, I threw myself at him at the end of it, and we both started to cry—he just a little, I quite a lot. It was a Sunday afternoon; he and my mother and I had gone for a walk in the botanical gardens. My mother had wandered off to look at some strange kind of thistle, and we could see her as she bent over the bushes to get a closer look and reach out to touch the leaves of the plant. When she returned to us and saw that we had both been crying, she started to get quite worked up, but my father quickly told her what had happened and she laughed at us and called us her little fools. But then she took me in her arms and kissed me, and she said that I needn't worry about such a thing as her sailing off or dying and leaving me all alone in the world. But if ever after that I saw my father sitting alone with a faraway look on his face, I was filled with pity for him. He had been alone in the world all that time, what with his mother sailing off on a boat with his father and his never seeing her again, and then his grandmother dying while lying next to him in the middle of the night. It was more than anyone should have to bear. I loved him so and wished that I had a mother to give him, for, no matter how much my own mother loved him, it could never be the same.

When my mother got through with the trunk, and I had heard again and again just what I had been like and who had said what to me at what point in my life, I was given my tea—a cup of cocoa and a buttered bun. My father by then would return home from work, and he was given his tea. As my mother went around preparing our supper, picking up clothes from the stone heap, or taking clothes off the clothesline, I would sit in a corner of our yard and watch her. She never stood still. Her powerful legs carried her from one part of the yard to the other, and in and out of the house. Sometimes she might call out to me to go and get some thyme or basil or some other herb for her, for she grew all her herbs in little pots that she kept in a corner of our little garden. Sometimes when I gave her the herbs, she might stoop down and kiss me on my lips and then on my neck. It was in such a paradise that I lived.

The summer of the year I turned twelve, I could see that I had grown taller; most of my clothes no longer fit. When I could get a dress over my head, the waist then came up to just below my chest. My legs had become more spindlelike, the hair on my head even more unruly than usual, small tufts of hair had appeared under my arms, and when I perspired the smell was strange, as if I had turned into a strange animal. I didn't say anything about it, and my mother and father didn't seem to notice, for they didn't say anything, either. Up to then, my mother and I had many dresses made out of the same cloth, though hers had a different, more grownup style, a boat neck or a sweetheart neckline, and a pleated or gored skirt, while my dresses had high necks with collars, a deep hemline, and, of course, a sash that tied in the back. One day, my mother and I had gone to get some material for new dresses to celebrate her birthday (the usual gift from my father), when I came upon a piece of cloth—a yellow background, with figures of men, dressed in a long-ago fashion, seated at pianos that they were playing, and all around them musical notes flying off into the air. I immediately said how much I loved this piece of cloth and how nice I thought it would look on us both, but my mother replied, "Oh, no. You are getting too old for that. It's time you had your own clothes. You just cannot go around the rest of your life looking like a little me." To say that I felt the earth swept away from under me would not be going too far. It wasn't just what she said, it was the way she said it. No accompanying little laugh. No bending over and kissing my little wet forehead (for suddenly I turned hot, then cold, and all my pores must have opened up, for fluids just flowed out of me). In the end, I got my dress with the men playing their pianos, and my mother got a dress with red and yellow overgrown hibiscus, but I was never able to wear my own dress or see my mother in hers without feeling bitterness and hatred, directed not so much toward my mother as toward, I suppose, life in general.

As if that were not enough, my mother informed me that I was on the verge of becoming a young lady, so there were quite a few things I would have to do differently. She didn't say exactly just what it was that made me on the verge of becoming a young lady, and I was so glad of that, because I didn't want to know. Behind a closed door, I stood naked in front of a mirror and looked at myself from head to toe. I was so long and bony that I more than filled up the mirror, and my small ribs pressed out against my skin. I tried to push my unruly hair down against my head so that it would lie flat, but as soon as I let it go it bounced up again. I could see the small tufts of hair under my arms. And then I got a good look at my nose. It had suddenly spread across my face, almost blotting out my cheeks, taking up my whole face, so that if I didn't know I was me standing there I would have wondered about that strange girl—and to think that only so recently my nose had been a small thing, the size of a rosebud. But what could I do? I thought of begging my mother to ask my father if he could build for me a set of clamps into which I could screw myself at night before I went to sleep and which would surely cut back on my growing. I was about to ask her this when I remembered that a few days earlier I had asked in my most pleasing, winning way for a look through the trunk. A person I did not recognize answered in a voice I did not recognize, "Absolutely not! You and I don't have time for that anymore." Again, did the ground wash out from under me? Again, the answer would have to be yes, and I wouldn't be going too far.

Because of this young-lady business, instead of days spent in perfect harmony with my mother, I trailing in her footsteps, she showering down on me her kisses and affection and attention, I was now sent off to learn one thing and another. I was sent to someone who knew all about manners and how to meet and greet important people in the world. This woman soon asked me not to come again, since I could not resist making farting-like noises each time I had to practice a curtsy, it made the other girls laugh so. I was sent for piano lessons. The piano teacher, a shriveled-up old spinster from Lancashire, England, soon asked me not to come back, since I seemed unable to resist eating from the bowl of plums she had placed on the piano purely for decoration. In the first case, I told my mother a lie—I told her that the manners teacher had found that my manners needed no improvement, so I needn't come anymore. This made her very pleased. In the second case, there was no getting around it—she had to find out. When the piano teacher told her of my misdeed, she turned and walked away from me, and I wasn't sure that if she had been asked who I was she wouldn't have said, "I don't know," right then and there. What a new thing this was for me: my mother's back turned on me in disgust. It was true that I didn't spend all my days at my mother's side before this, that I spent most of my days at school, but before this young-lady business I could sit and think of my mother, see her doing one thing or another, and always her face bore a smile for me. Now I often saw her with the corners of her mouth turned down in disapproval of me. And why was my mother carrying my new state so far? She took to pointing out that one day I would have my own house and I might want it to be a different house from the one she kept. Once, when showing me a way to store linen, she patted the folded sheets in place and said, "Of course, in your own house you might choose another way." That the day might actually come when we would live apart I had never believed. My throat hurt from the tears I held bottled up tight inside. Sometimes we would both forget the new order of things and would slip into our old ways. But that didn't last very long.

In the middle of all these new things, I had forgotten that I was to enter a new school that September. I had then a set of things to do, preparing for school. I had to go to the seamstress to be measured for new uniforms, since my body now made a mockery of the old measurements. I had to get shoes, a new school hat, and lots of new books. In my new school, I needed a different exercise book for each subject, and in addition to the usual—English, arithmetic, and so on—I now had to take Latin and French, and attend classes in a brand-new science building. I began to look forward to my new school. I hoped that everyone there would be new, that there would be no one I had ever met before. That way, I could put on a new set of airs; I could say I was something that I was not, and no one would ever know the difference. On the Sunday before the Monday I started at my new school, my mother became cross over the way I had made my bed. In the center of my bedspread, my mother had embroidered a bowl overflowing with flowers and two lovebirds on either side of the bowl. I had placed the bedspread on my bed in a lopsided way so that the embroidery was not in the center of my bed, the way it should have been. My mother made a fuss about it, and I could see that she was right and I regretted very much not doing that one little thing that would have pleased her. I had lately become careless, she said, and I could only silently agree with her.

I came home from church, and my mother still seemed to hold the bedspread against me, so I kept out of her way. At half past two in the afternoon, I went off to Sunday school. At Sunday school, I was given a certificate for best student in my study-of-the-Bible group. It was a surprise that I would receive the certificate on that day, though we had known about the results of a test weeks before. I rushed home with my certificate in hand, feeling that with this prize I would reconquer my mother—a chance for her to smile on me again.

When I got to our house, I rushed into the yard and called out to her, but no answer came. I then walked into the house. At first, I didn't hear anything. Then I heard sounds coming from the direction of my parents' room. My mother must be in there, I thought. When I got to the door, I could see that my mother and father were lying in their bed. It didn't interest me what they were doing—only that my mother's hand was on the small of my father's back and that it was making a circular motion. But her hand! It was white and bony, as if it had long been dead and had been left out in the elements. It seemed not to be her hand, and yet it could only be her hand, so well did I know it. It went around and around in the same circular motion, and I looked at it as if I would never see anything else in my life again. If I were to forget everything else in the world, I could not forget her hand as it looked then. I could also make out that the sounds I had heard were her kissing my father's ears and his mouth and his face. I looked at them for I don't know how long.

When I next saw my mother, I was standing at the dinner table that I had just set, having made a tremendous commotion with knives and forks as I got them out of their drawer, letting my parents know that I was home. I had set the table and was now half standing near my chair, half draped over the table, staring at nothing in particular and trying to ignore my mother's presence. Though I couldn't remember our eyes having met, I was quite sure that she had seen me in the bedroom, and I didn't know what I would say if she mentioned it. Instead, she said in a voice that was sort of cross and sort of something else, "Are you going to just stand there doing nothing all day?" The something else was new; I had never heard it in her voice before. I couldn't say exactly what it was, but I know that it caused me to reply, "And what if I do?" and at the same time to stare at her directly in the eyes. It must have been a shock to her, the way I spoke. I had never talked back to her before. She looked at me, and then, instead of saying some squelching thing that would put me back in my place, she dropped her eyes and walked away. From the back, she looked small and funny. She carried her hands limp at her sides. I was sure I could never let those hands touch me again; I was sure I could never let her kiss me again. All that was finished.

I was amazed that I could eat my food, for all of it reminded me of things that had taken place between my mother and me. A long time ago, when I wouldn't eat my beef, complaining that it involved too much chewing, my mother would first chew up pieces of meat in her own mouth and then feed it to me. When I had hated carrots so much that even the sight of them would send me into a fit of tears, my mother would try to find all sorts of ways to make them palatable for me. All that was finished now. I didn't think that I would ever think of any of it again with fondness. I looked at my parents. My father was just the same, eating his food in the same old way, his two rows of false teeth clop-clopping like a horse being driven off to market. He was regaling us with another one of his stories about when he was a young man and played cricket on one island or the other. What he said now must have been funny, for my mother couldn't stop laughing. He didn't seem to notice that I was not entertained.

My father and I then went for our customary Sunday-afternoon walk. My mother did not come with us. I don't know what she stayed home to do. On our walk, my father tried to hold my hand, but I pulled myself away from him, doing it in such a way that he would think I felt too big for that now.

That Monday, I went to my new school. I was placed in a class with girls I had never seen before.

Some of them had heard about me, though, for I was the youngest among them and was said to be very bright. I liked a girl named Albertine, and I liked a girl named Gweneth. At the end of the day, Gwen and I were in love, and so we walked home arm in arm together.

When I got home, my mother greeted me with the customary kiss and inquiries. I told her about my day, going out of my way to provide pleasing details, leaving out, of course, any mention at all of Gwen and my overpowering feelings for her.

Chapter Three

Gwen

On opening day, I walked to my new school alone. It was the first and last time that such a thing would happen. All around me were other people my age—twelve years—girls and boys, dressed in their school uniforms, marching off to school. They all seemed to know each other, and as they met they would burst into laughter, slapping each other on the shoulder and back, telling each other things that must have made for much happiness. I saw some girls wearing the same uniform as my own, and my heart just longed for them to say something to me, but the most they could do to include me was to smile and nod in my direction as they walked on arm in arm. I could hardly blame them for not paying more attention to me. Everything about me was so new: my uniform was new, my shoes were new, my hat was new, my shoulder ached from the weight of my new books in my new bag; even the road I walked on was

new, and I must have put my feet down as if I weren't
sure the ground was solid. At school, the yard was
filled with more of these girls and their most sure-of-
themselves gaits. When I looked at them, they made
up a sea. They were walking in and out among the
beds of flowers, all across the fields, all across the
courtyard, in and out of classrooms. Except for me,
no one seemed a stranger to anything or anyone.
Hearing the way they greeted each other, I couldn't
be sure that they hadn't all come out of the same
woman's belly, and at the same time, too. Looking at
them, I was suddenly glad that because I had wanted
to avoid an argument with my mother I had eaten all
my breakfast, for now I surely would have fainted if
I had been in any more weakened a condition.

I knew where my classroom was, because my
mother and I had kept an appointment at the school
a week before. There I met some of my teachers and
was shown the ins and outs of everything. When I
saw it then, it was nice and orderly and empty and
smelled just scrubbed. Now it smelled of girls milling around, fresh ink in inkwells, new books, chalk
and erasers. The girls in my classroom acted even
more familiar with each other. I was sure I would
never be able to tell them apart just from looking
at them, and I was sure that I would never be able to
tell them apart from the sound of their voices.

When the school bell rang at half past eight, we
formed ourselves into the required pairs and filed
into the auditorium for morning prayers and hymn-
singing. Our headmistress gave us a little talk, wel-

coming the new students and welcoming back the old students, saying that she hoped we had all left our bad ways behind us, that we would be good examples for each other and bring greater credit to our school than any of the other groups of girls who had been there before us. My palms were wet, and quite a few times the ground felt as if it were seesawing under my feet, but that didn't stop me from taking in a few things. For instance, the headmistress, Miss Moore. I knew right away that she had come to Antigua from England, for she looked like a prune left out of its jar a long time and she sounded as if she had borrowed her voice from an owl. The way she said, "Now, girls . . ." When she was just standing still there, listening to some of the other activities, her gray eyes going all around the room hoping to see something wrong, her throat would beat up and down as if a fish fresh out of water were caught inside. I wondered if she even smelled like a fish. Once when I didn't wash, my mother had given me a long scolding about it, and she ended by saying that it was the only thing she didn't like about English people: they didn't wash often enough, or wash properly when they finally did. My mother had said, "Have you ever noticed how they smell as if they had been bottled up in a fish?" On either side of Miss Moore stood our other teachers, women and men—mostly women. I recognized Miss George, our music teacher; Miss Nelson, our home-room teacher; Miss Edward, our history and geography teacher; and Miss Newgate, our algebra and geometry teacher. I had met them the day my mother and I were at school. I did not know who the others were, and I did not worry about it. Since they were teachers, I was sure it wouldn't be long before, because of some misunderstanding, they would be thorns in my side.

We walked back to our classroom the same way we had come, quite orderly and, except for a few whispered exchanges, quite silent. But no sooner were we back in our classroom than the girls were in each other's laps, arms wrapped around necks. After peeping over my shoulder left and right, I sat down in my seat and wondered what would become of me. There were twenty of us in my class, and we were seated at desks arranged five in a row, four rows deep. I was at a desk in the third row, and this made me even more miserable. I hated to be seated so far away from the teacher, because I was sure I would miss something she said. But, even worse, if I was out of my teacher's sight all the time, how could she see my industriousness and quickness at learning things? And, besides, only dunces were seated so far to the rear, and I could not bear to be thought a dunce. I was now staring at the back of a shrubby-haired girl seated in the front row—the seat I most coveted, since it was directly in front of the teacher's desk. At that moment, the girl twisted herself around, stared at me, and said, "You are Annie John? We hear you are very bright." It was a good thing Miss Nelson walked in right then, for how would it have appeared if I had replied, "Yes, that is completely true"—the very thing that was on the tip of my tongue.

As soon as Miss Nelson walked in, we came to order and stood up stiffly at our desks. She said to us, "Good morning, class," half in a way that someone must have told her was the proper way to speak to us and half in a jocular way, as if we secretly amused her. We replied, "Good morning, Miss," in unison and in a respectful way, at the same time making a barely visible curtsy, also in unison. When she had seated herself at her desk, she said to us, "You may sit now," and we did. She opened the roll book, and as she called out our names each of us answered, "Present, Miss." As she called out our names, she kept her head bent over the book, but when she called out my name and I answered with the customary response she looked up and smiled at me and said, "Welcome, Annie." Everyone, of course, then turned and looked at me. I was sure it was because they could hear the loud racket my heart was making in my chest.

It was the first day of a new term, Miss Nelson said, so we would not be attending to any of our usual subjects; instead, we were to spend the morning in contemplation and reflection and writing something she described as an "autobiographical essay." In the afternoon, we would read aloud to each other our autobiographical essays. (I knew quite well about "autobiography" and "essay," but reflection and contemplation! A day at school spent in such a way! Of course, in most books all the good people were always contemplating and reflecting before they did anything. Perhaps in her mind's eye she could see our futures and, against all prediction, we turned out to be good people.) On hearing this, a huge sigh went up from the girls. Half the sighs were in happiness at the thought of sitting and gazing off into clear space, the other half in unhappiness at the misdeeds that would have to go unaccomplished. I joined the happy half, because I knew it would please Miss Nelson, and, my own selfish interest aside, I liked so much the way she wore her ironed hair and her long-sleeved blouse and box-pleated skirt that I wanted to please her.

The morning was uneventful enough: a girl spilled ink from her inkwell all over her uniform; a girl broke her pen nib and then made a big to-do about replacing it; girls twisted and turned in their seats and pinched each other's bottoms; girls passed notes to each other. All this Miss Nelson must have seen and heard, but she didn't say anything—only kept reading her book: an elaborately illustrated edition of *The Tempest*, as later, passing by her desk, I saw. Midway in the morning, we were told to go out and stretch our legs and breathe some fresh air for a few minutes; when we returned, we were given glasses of cold lemonade and a slice of bun to refresh us.

As soon as the sun stood in the middle of the sky, we were sent home for lunch. The earth may have grown an inch or two larger between the time I had walked to school that morning and the time I went home to lunch, for some girls made a small space for me in their little band. But I couldn't pay much attention to them; my mind was on my new surroundings, my new teacher, what I had written in my nice new notebook with its black-all-mixed-up-with-white cover and smooth lined pages (so glad was I to get rid of my old notebooks, which had on their covers a picture of a wrinkled-up woman wearing a crown on her head and a neckful and armfuls of diamonds and pearls—their pages so coarse, as if they were made of cornmeal). I flew home. I must have eaten my food. I flew back to school. By half past one, we were sitting under a flamboyant tree in a secluded part of our schoolyard, our autobiographical essays in hand. We were about to read aloud what we had written during our morning of contemplation and reflection.

In response to Miss Nelson, each girl stood up and read her composition. One girl told of a much revered and loved aunt who now lived in England and of how much she looked forward to one day moving to England to live with her aunt; one girl told of her brother studying medicine in Canada and the life she imagined he lived there (it seemed quite odd to me); one girl told of the fright she had when she dreamed she was dead, and of the matching fright she had when she woke and found that she wasn't (everyone laughed at this, and Miss Nelson had to call us to order over and over); one girl told of how her oldest sister's best friend's cousin's best friend (it was a real rigmarole) had gone on a Girl Guide jamboree held in Trinidad and met someone who millions of years ago had taken tea with Lady Baden-Powell; one girl told of an excursion she and her father had made to

Redonda, and of how they had seen some booby birds tending their chicks. Things went on in that way, all so playful, all so imaginative. I began to wonder about what I had written, for it was the opposite of playful and it was the opposite of imaginative. What I had written was heartfelt, and, except for the very end, it was all too true. The afternoon was wearing itself thin. Would my turn ever come? What should I do, finding myself in a world of new girls, a world in which I was not even near the center?

It was a while before I realized that Miss Nelson was calling on me. My turn at last to read what I had written. I got up and started to read, my voice shaky at first, but since the sound of my own voice had always been a calming potion to me, it wasn't long before I was reading in such a way that, except for the chirp of some birds, the hum of bees looking for flowers, the silvery rush-rush of the wind in the trees, the only sound to be heard was my voice as it rose and fell in sentence after sentence. At the end of my reading, I thought I was imagining the upturned faces on which were looks of adoration, but I was not; I thought I was imagining, too, some eyes brimming over with tears, but again I was not. Miss Nelson said that she would like to borrow what I had written to read for herself, and that it would be placed on the shelf with the books that made up our own class library, so that it would be available to any girl who wanted to read it. This is what I had written:

"When I was a small child, my mother and I used to go down to Rat Island on Sundays right after church, so that I could bathe in the sea. It was at a time when I was thought to have weak kidneys and a bath in the sea had been recommended as a strengthening remedy. Rat Island wasn't a place many people went to anyway, but by climbing down some rocks my mother had found a place that nobody seemed to have ever been. Since this bathing in the sea was a medicine and not a picnic, we had to bathe without wearing swimming costumes. My mother was a superior swimmer. When she plunged into the seawater, it was as if she had always lived there. She would go far out if it was safe to do so, and she could tell just by looking at the way the waves beat if it was safe to do so. She could tell if a shark was nearby, and she had never been stung by a jellyfish. I, on the other hand, could not swim at all. In fact, if I was in water up to my knees I was sure that I was drowning. My mother had tried everything to get me swimming, from using a coaxing method to just throwing me without a word into the water. Nothing worked. The only way I could go into the water was if I was on my mother's back, my arms clasped tightly around her neck, and she would then swim around not too far from the shore. It was only then that I could forget how big the sea was, how far down the bottom could be, and how filled up it was with things that couldn't understand a nice hallo. When we swam around in this way, I would think how much we were like the pictures of sea mammals I had seen, my mother and I, naked in the seawater, my mother sometimes singing to me a song in a French patois I did not yet

understand, or sometimes not saying anything at all.
I would place my ear against her neck, and it was as if
I were listening to a giant shell, for all the sounds
around me—the sea, the wind, the birds screeching—
would seem as if they came from inside her, the way
the sounds of the sea are in a seashell. Afterward, my
mother would take me back to the shore, and I would
lie there just beyond the farthest reach of a big wave
and watch my mother as she swam and dove.

"One day, in the midst of watching my mother
swim and dive, I heard a commotion far out at sea.
It was three ships going by, and they were filled with
people. They must have been celebrating something,
for the ships would blow their horns and the people
would cheer in response. After they passed out of
view, I turned back to look at my mother, but I could
not see her. My eyes searched the small area of water
where she should have been, but I couldn't find her.
I stood up and started to call out her name, but no
sound would come out of my throat. A huge black
space then opened up in front of me and I fell inside it.
I couldn't see what was in front of me and I couldn't
hear anything around me. I couldn't think of anything except that my mother was no longer near me.
Things went on in this way for I don't know how long.
I don't know what, but something drew my eye in
one direction. A little bit out of the area in which she
usually swam was my mother, just sitting and tracing
patterns on a large rock. She wasn't paying any attention to me, for she didn't know that I had missed her.
I was glad to see her and started jumping up and

down and waving to her. Still she didn't see me, and then I started to cry, for it dawned on me that, with all that water between us and I being unable to swim, my mother could stay there forever and the only way I would be able to wrap my arms around her again was if it pleased her or if I took a boat. I cried until I wore myself out. My tears ran down into my mouth, and it was the first time that I realized tears had a bitter and salty taste. Finally, my mother came ashore. She was, of course, alarmed when she saw my face, for I had let the tears just dry there and they left a stain. When I told her what had happened, she hugged me so close that it was hard to breathe, and she told me that nothing could be farther from the truth—that she would never ever leave me. And though she said it over and over again, and though I felt better, I could not wipe out of my mind the feeling I had had when I couldn't find her.

"The summer just past, I kept having a dream about my mother sitting on the rock. Over and over I would have the dream—only in it my mother never came back, and sometimes my father would join her. When he joined her, they would both sit tracing patterns on the rock, and it must have been amusing, for they would always make each other laugh. At first, I didn't say anything, but when I began to have the dream again and again, I finally told my mother. My mother became instantly distressed; tears came to her eyes, and, taking me in her arms, she told me all the same things she had told me on the day at the sea, and this time the memory of the dark time when I felt I would never see her again did not come back to haunt me."

I didn't exactly tell a lie about the last part. That is just what would have happened in the old days. But actually the past year saw me launched into young-ladyness, and when I told my mother of my dream— my nightmare, really—I was greeted with a turned back and a warning against eating certain kinds of fruit in an unripe state just before going to bed. I placed the old days' version before my classmates because, I thought, I couldn't bear to show my mother in a bad light before people who hardly knew her. But the real truth was that I couldn't bear to have anyone see how deep in disfavor I was with my mother.

As we walked back to the classroom, I in the air, my classmates on the ground, jostling each other to say some words of appreciation and congratulation to me, my head felt funny, as if it had swelled up to the size of, and weighed no more than, a blown-up balloon. Often I had been told by my mother not to feel proud of anything I had done and in the next breath that I couldn't feel enough pride about something I had done. Now I tossed from one to the other: my head bowed down to the ground, my head high up in the air. I looked at these girls surrounding me, my heart filled with just-sprung-up love, and I wished then and there to spend the rest of my life only with them.

As we approached our classroom, I felt a pinch on my arm. It was an affectionate pinch, I could tell. It was the girl who had earlier that day asked me if my name was Annie John. Now she told me that her name was Gweneth Joseph, and reaching into the pocket of her tunic, she brought out a small rock and presented it to me. She had found it, she said, at the foot of a sleeping volcano. The rock was black, and it felt rough in my hands, as if it had been through a lot. I immediately put it to my nose to see what it smelled like. It smelled of lavender, because Gweneth Joseph had kept it wrapped in a handkerchief doused in that scent. It may have been in that moment that we fell in love. Later, we could never agree on when it was. That afternoon, we walked home together, she going a little out of her usual way, and we exchanged likes and dislikes, our jaws dropping and eyes widening when we saw how similar they were. We separated ourselves from the other girls, and they, understanding everything, left us alone. We cut through a tamarind grove, we cut through a cherry-tree grove, we passed down the lane where all the houses had elaborate hedges growing in front, so that nothing was visible but the upstairs windows. When we came to my street, parting was all but unbearable. "Tomorrow," we said, to cheer each other up.

Gwen and I were soon inseparable. If you saw one, you saw the other. For me, each day began as I waited for Gwen to come by and fetch me for school. My heart beat fast as I stood in the front yard of our house waiting to see Gwen as she rounded the bend in our street. The sun, already way up in the sky so early in the morning, shone on her, and the whole street became suddenly empty so that Gwen and everything about her were perfect, as if she were in a picture. Her panama hat, with the navy blue and gold satin ribbon—our school colors—around the brim, sat lopsided on her head, for her head was small and she never seemed to get the correct-size hat, and it had to be anchored with a piece of elastic running under her chin. The pleats in the tunic of her uniform were in place, as was to be expected. Her cotton socks fit neatly around her ankles, and her shoes shone from just being polished. If a small breeze blew, it would ruffle the ribbons in her short, shrubby hair and the hem of her tunic; if the hem of her tunic was disturbed in that way, I would then be able to see her knees. She had bony knees and they were always ash-colored, as if she had just finished giving them a good scratch or had just finished saying her prayers. The breeze might also blow back the brim of her hat, and since she always walked with her head held down I might then be able to see her face: a small, flattish nose; lips the shape of a saucer broken evenly in two; wide, high cheekbones; ears pinned back close against her head—which was always set in a serious way, as if she were going over in her mind some of the many things we had hit upon that were truly a mystery to us. (Though once I told her that about her face, and she said that really she had only been thinking about me. I didn't look to make sure, but I felt as if my whole skin had become covered with millions of tiny red boils and that shortly I would explode with happiness.) When finally she reached me, she would look up and we would both smile and say softly, "Hi." We'd set off for school side by side, our feet in step, not touching but feeling as if we were joined at the shoulder, hip, and ankle, not to mention heart.

As we walked together, we told each other things we had judged most private and secret: things we had overheard our parents say, dreams we had had the night before, the things we were really afraid of; but especially we told of our love for each other. Except for the ordinary things that naturally came up, I never told her about my changed feeling for my mother. I could see in what high regard Gwen held me, and I couldn't bear for her to see the great thing I had had once and then lost without an explanation. By the time we got to school, our chums often seemed overbearing, with their little comments on the well-pressedness of each other's uniforms, or on the neatness of their schoolbooks, or on how much they approved of the way Miss Nelson was wearing her hair these days. A few other girls were having much the same experience as Gwen and I, and when we heard comments of this kind we would look at each other and roll up our eyes and toss our hands in the air—a way of saying how above such concerns we were. The gesture was an exact copy, of course, of what we had seen our mothers do.

My life in school became just the opposite of my first morning. I went from being ignored, with hardly a glance from anyone, to having girls vie for my friendship, or at least for more than just a passing acquaintanceship. Both my classmates and my teachers noticed how quick I was at learning things. I was soon given responsibility for overseeing the class in the teacher's absence. At first, I was a little taken aback by this, but then I got used to it. I indulged many things, especially if they would end in a laugh or something touching. I would never dillydally with a decision, always making up my mind right away about the thing in front of me. Sometimes, seeing my old frail self in a girl, I would defend her; sometimes, seeing my old frail self in a girl, I would be heartless and cruel. It all went over quite well, and I became very popular.

My so recently much-hated body was now a plus: I excelled at games and was named captain of a volleyball team. As I was favored by my classmates inside and outside the classroom, so was I favored by my teachers—though only inside the classroom, for I had become notorious to them for doing forbidden things. If sometimes I stood away from myself and took a look at who I had become, I couldn't be more surprised at what I saw. But since who I had become earned me the love and devotion of Gwen and the other girls, I was only egged on to find new and better ways to entertain them. I don't know what invisible standard was set, or by whom or exactly when, but eight of us met it, and soon to the other girls we were something to comment on favorably or unfavorably, as the case might be.

It was in a nook of some old tombstones—a place

discovered by girls going to our school long before we were born—shaded by trees with trunks so thick it would take four arm's lengths to encircle them, that we would sit and talk about the things we said were on our minds that day. On our minds every day were our breasts and their refusal to budge out of our chests. On hearing somewhere that if a boy rubbed your breasts they would quickly swell up, I passed along this news. Since in the world we occupied and hoped forever to occupy boys were banished, we had to make do with ourselves. What perfection we found in each other, sitting on these tombstones of long-dead people who had been the masters of our ancestors! Nothing in particular really troubled us except for the annoyance of a fly colliding with our lips, sticky from eating fruits; a bee wanting to nestle in our hair; the breeze suddenly blowing too strong. We were sure that the much-talked-about future that everybody was preparing us for would never come, for we had such a powerful feeling against it, and why shouldn't our will prevail this time? Sometimes when we looked at each other, it was all we could do not to cry out with happiness.

My own special happiness was, of course, with Gwen. She would stand in front of me trying to see into my murky black eyes—a way, she said, to tell exactly what I was thinking. After a short while, she would give up, saying, "I can't make out a thing— only my same old face." I would then laugh at her and kiss her on the neck, sending her into a fit of shivers, as if someone had exposed her to a cold draft

when she had a fever. Sometimes when she spoke to
me, so overcome with feeling would I be that I was
no longer able to hear what she said, I could only
make out her mouth as it moved up and down. I
told her that I wished I had been named Enid, after
Enid Blyton, the author of the first books I had
discovered on my own and liked. I told her that when
I was younger I had been afraid of my mother's dying, but that since I had met Gwen this didn't matter
so much. Whenever I spoke of my mother to her, I
was always sure to turn the corners of my mouth
down, to show my scorn. I said that I could not wait
for us to grow up so that we could live in a house of
our own. I had already picked out the house. It was
a gray one, with many rooms, and it was in the lane
where all the houses had high, well-trimmed hedges.
With all my plans she agreed, and I am sure that if
she had had any plans of her own I would have agreed
with them also.

On the morning of the first day I started to
menstruate, I felt strange in a new way—hot and cold
at the same time, with horrible pains running up and
down my legs. My mother, knowing what was the
matter, brushed aside my complaints and said that it
was all to be expected and I would soon get used to
everything. Seeing my gloomy face, she told me in a
half-joking way all about her own experience with
the first step in coming of age, as she called it, which
had happened when she was as old as I was. I pre-
tended that this information made us close—as close

as in the old days—but to myself I said, "What a serpent!"

I walked to school with Gwen feeling as I supposed a dog must feel when it has done something wrong and is ashamed of itself and trying to get somewhere quick, where it can lie low. The cloth between my legs grew heavier and heavier with every step I took, and I was sure that everything about me broadcast, "She's menstruating today. She's menstruating today." When Gwen heard what had happened, tears came to her eyes. She had not yet had the wonderful experience, and I could see that she cried for herself. She said that, in sympathy, she would wear a cloth, too.

In class, for the first time in my life, I fainted. Miss Nelson had to revive me, passing her smelling salts, which she had in a beautiful green vial, back and forth under my nose. She then took me to Nurse, who said that it was the fright of all the unexpected pain that had caused me to faint, but I knew that I had fainted after I brought to my mind a clear picture of myself sitting at my desk in my own blood.

At recess, among the tombstones, I of course had to exhibit and demonstrate. None of the others were menstruating yet. I showed everything without the least bit of flourish, since my heart wasn't in it. I wished instead that one of the other girls were in my place and that I were just sitting there in amazement. How nice they all were, though, rallying to my side, offering shoulders on which to lean, laps in which to rest my weary, aching head, and kisses that really did soothe. When I looked at them sitting around me, the church in the distance, beyond that our school, with throngs of girls crossing back and forth in the schoolyard, beyond that the world, how I wished that everything would fall away, so that suddenly we'd be sitting in some different atmosphere, with no future full of ridiculous demands, no need for any sustenance save our love for each other, with no hindrance to any of our desires, which would, of course, be simple desires—nothing, nothing, just sitting on our tombstones forever. But that could never be, as the tolling of the school bell testified.

We walked back to class slowly, as if going to a funeral. Gwen and I vowed to love each other always, but the words had a hollow ring, and when we looked at each other we couldn't sustain the gaze. It had been decided by Miss Nelson and Nurse that I was not to return to school after lunch, with Nurse sending instructions to my mother to keep me in bed for the rest of the day.

When I got home, my mother came toward me, arms outstretched, concern written on her face. My whole mouth filled up with a bitter taste, for I could not understand how she could be so beautiful even though I no longer loved her.

Chapter Four

The Red Girl

I always slammed the gate to our yard behind me when I was up to something. If I was leaving the house, the slam was to let my mother know that I had left, so she could stop worrying about me and put her mind on something else. Then, after a proper time had passed, I would quietly unlatch the gate, creep back into the yard, and dive under the house to extract or hide some object that was forbidden me— usually some object that had come into my possession through my expert stealing. If I was returning home, I would reverse this procedure, first being very quiet, checking my things under the house, making sure that everything was still in place, often adding a new treasure; then the loud bang of the gate to announce to my mother that I had only just then returned home. My mother would usually say, "How many times do I have to tell you not to slam the gate?"

I had under the house almost all the books I had ever read. After reading a book, whether I liked it or not, I couldn't bear to part with it. I would then steal it. I was always successful, because casting suspicion away from me and putting on an innocent face had become a specialty of mine. I had a few books that I had received in the usual straightforward way, for birthdays and Christmas, and as prizes in school; these were all displayed on a little shelf my father had built for me, and whenever I felt I was falling out of my mother's good graces I would let her see me absorbed in these books. She would come over and caress my forehead, kiss me, and say, "I know how you like to read, but you mustn't strain your eyes." Feeling the slate wiped clean, I would then plot something new.

It was my mother who gave me my first marbles. They had come, a pair of them, as a bonus in a box of oats, and she thought that their unusual size—they were as big as plums—and their color would amuse me. One was white with blue, the other white with a brownish yellow. They looked to me like miniature globes, the white representing the seas, the colors representing land masses. I didn't think very much of them as I rolled them around in my palms, but my mother, taking the brownish-yellow one in her hand and holding it up in the air, said, "What a nice color! Amber." Amber! Needless to say, when I showed the marbles to my friends at school I said, "Such a nice color, amber," causing the desired effect among them, for on hearing me say the word "amber" they widened their eyes and shaped their mouths into tiny "o"s.

One day, I was throwing stones at a guava tree, trying to knock down a ripe guava, when the Red Girl came along and said, "Which one do you want?" After I pointed it out, she climbed up the tree, picked the one I wanted off its branch, climbed down, and presented it to me. How my eyes did widen and my mouth form an "o" at this. I had never seen a girl do this before. All the boys climbed trees for the fruit they wanted, and all the girls threw stones to knock the fruit off the trees. But look at the way she climbed that tree: better than any boy.

Polishing off the delicious ripe-to-perfection guava in two bites, I took a good look at the Red Girl. How right I had been to take some special notice of her the first time I had seen her. She was holding on to her mother's skirt and I was holding on to my mother's skirt. Our mothers waved to each other as they passed, calling out the usual greetings, making the usual inquiries. I noticed that the girl's hair was the color of a penny fresh from the mint, and that it was so unruly it had to be forcibly twisted into corkscrews, the ends tied tightly with white thread. The corkscrews didn't lie flat on her head, they stood straight up, and when she walked they bounced up and down as if they were something amphibian and alive. Right away to myself I called her the Red Girl. For as she passed, in my mind's eye I could see her surrounded by flames, the house she lived in on fire, and she could not escape. I rescued her, and after that she followed me around worshipfully and took with great forbearance any and every abuse I heaped on her. I would have gone on like that for a while, but my mother tugged at me, claiming my attention; I heard her say, "Such a nice woman, to keep that girl so dirty."

The Red Girl and I stood under the guava tree looking each other up and down. What a beautiful thing I saw standing before me. Her face was big and round and red, like a moon—a red moon. She had big, broad, flat feet, and they were naked to the bare ground; her dress was dirty, the skirt and blouse tearing away from each other at one side; the red hair that I had first seen standing up on her head was matted and tangled; her hands were big and fat, and her fingernails held at least ten anthills of dirt under them. And on top of that, she had such an unbelievable, wonderful smell, as if she had never taken a bath in her whole life.

I soon learned this about her: She took a bath only once a week, and that was only so that she could be admitted to her grandmother's presence. She didn't like to bathe, and her mother didn't force her. She changed her dress once a week for the same reason. She preferred to wear a dress until it just couldn't be worn anymore. Her mother didn't mind that, either. She didn't like to comb her hair, though on the first day of school she could put herself out for that. She didn't like to go to Sunday school, and her mother didn't force her. She didn't like to brush her teeth, but occasionally her mother said it was necessary. She loved to play marbles, and was so good that only Skerritt boys now played against her. Oh, what an angel she was, and what a heaven she lived in! I, on the other hand, took a full bath every morning and a sponge bath every night. I could hardly go out on my doorstep without putting my shoes on. I was not allowed to play in the sun without a hat on my head. My mother paid a woman who lived five houses away from us sevenpence a week—a penny for each school day and twopence for Sunday—to comb my hair. On Saturday, my mother washed my hair. Before I went to sleep at night, I had to make sure my uniform was clean and creaseless and all laid out for the next day. I had to make sure that my shoes were clean and polished to a nice shine. I went to Sunday school every Sunday unless I was sick. I was not allowed to play marbles, and, as for Skerritt boys, that was hardly mentionable.

The Red Girl and I walked to the top of the hill behind my house. At the top of the hill was an old lighthouse. It must have been a useful lighthouse at one time, but now it was just there for mothers to say to their children, "Don't play at the lighthouse," my own mother leading the chorus, I am sure. Whenever I did go to the lighthouse behind my mother's back, I would have to gather up all my courage to go to the top, the height made me so dizzy. But now I marched boldly up behind the Red Girl as if at the

top were my own room, with all my familiar com-
forts waiting for me. At the top, we stood on the
balcony and looked out toward the sea. We could see
some boats coming and going; we could see some
children our own age coming home from games; we
could see some sheep being driven home from pasture; we could see my father coming home from work.

It went without saying between us that my mother
should never know that we had become friends, that
we planned to meet at the lighthouse in this way every
day for the rest of our lives and beyond, that I now
worshipped the ground her unwashed feet walked on.
Just before we parted, she gave me three marbles;
they were an ordinary kind, the kind you could buy
three for a penny—glass orbs with a tear-shaped drop
suspended in the center. Another secret to keep from
my mother!

And now I started a new series of betrayals of
people and things I would have sworn only minutes
before to die for. There was Gweneth, whom I loved
so, and who was my dearest friend in spite of the
fact that she met with my mother's complete approval, but she had such slyness and so many pleasing, to me, ways that my mother could never have
imagined. There she was, waiting for me in our usual
spot behind the cistern. "Oh, Gwen, wait until I tell
you this," I would begin after we had embraced and
exchanged kisses. We would then bring each other up
to date on all our latest triumphs and disappoint-
ments. But now, as my head rested on her shoulder,

I thought how dull was the fresh pressedness of her uniform, the cleanness of her neck, the neatness of her just combed plaits. We walked into our classroom in the usual way, arm in arm—her head on *my* shoulder, since I was the taller—identical smiles on our faces. The Little Lovebirds, our friends called us. Who could have guessed at that moment about the new claim on my heart? Certainly not Gwen. For, of course, in bringing her up to date I never mentioned the Red Girl.

As for the marbles! Quite by accident, in a moment when I was just fooling about, I discovered that I had a talent for playing marbles. I played a game and I won. I played another game and I won. I took winning for a sign of the perfection of my new union with the Red Girl. I devoted my spare time to playing and winning marbles. No longer could I head a side for a game of rounders; no longer could I, during a break for recess, walk over from our schoolyard into the neighboring churchyard to sit on tombstones and gather important information from the other girls on what exactly it was I should do to make my breasts begin growing. Our breasts were, to us, treasured shrubs, needing only the proper combination of water and sunlight to make them flourish. All my free time became devoted to games of marbles. And how I won! From the day I went to school with the three gifts from the Red Girl and came home that same day with twenty—enough to fill an old one-pound tin. Everyone attributed my talent to my long arms and my steady gaze. What a surprise it was to me—something about myself I had not known. Perhaps it had stuck in my mind that once my mother said to me, "I am so glad you are not one of those girls who like to play marbles," and perhaps because I had to do exactly the opposite of whatever she desired of me, I now played and played at marbles in a way that I had never done anything. Soon I had so many marbles that I had to store them in old containers, hiding them under the house in places where they would not be readily visible if my mother should just one day stoop down and make a sweeping search with her ever-inquisitive, ever-sharp eyes. If I had not yet come up with the trick of slamming the gate, I would surely have come up with it now. Sometimes I slammed the gate so hard that even I began to be afraid it would come off its hinges.

At first, the Red Girl and I met every day. Every day after I finished my chores, each chore being a small rehearsal for that faraway day, thank God, when I would be the mistress of my own house, that faraway day when I would have to abandon Gwen, the Red Girl, meetings behind cistern and at lighthouse, marbles, places under the house, and every other secret pleasure. I would say to my mother, "I think I will just go and stretch my legs a bit." It didn't take her very long to wonder why, after all my daily activities, I should suddenly have an urge to stretch my legs. She said to me, "Why, after all the things you do every day, the sudden urge to have your legs stretched?" I had always been extremely lazy, enjoying nothing so much as lying on my bed, my legs resting on the windowsill, to catch the hot sun, reading one of my books, stolen or otherwise, or just toying with another treasure. After my mother said this, I stopped going to the lighthouse for a few days, and I worried about how to explain this interference to the Red Girl. How convenient for me it would be, I thought, to have a mother to whom I was not a prime interest. But I found a new tack. A few days later, I told my mother that for my drawing class I had been asked to observe a field at sunset, so that in class I could reproduce it in watercolors; would it be all right, then, if I just went for a small walk up and over the hill? The question was framed in just the way I knew it would appeal to her, so eager was she to contribute to my scholarship. Of course she agreed. My feet must have had wings; in seconds, I was at the top of the lighthouse.

All the time I had been kept prisoner under the watchful gaze of my mother, the Red Girl had faithfully gone to our meeting place every day. Every day, she went and waited for me, and every day I failed to show up. What could I say to her now? "My mother, the Nosy Parker, would kill me—or, worse, not speak to me for at least a few hours—if she knew that I met you in a secret place," I said. For a while after I got there, we said nothing, only staring out to sea, watching the boats coming and going, watching the children our own age coming home from games, watching the sheep being driven home from pasture. Then, still without saying a word, the Red Girl began to pinch me. She pinched hard, picking up pieces of my almost nonexistent flesh and twisting it around. At first, I vowed not to cry, but it went on for so long that tears I could not control streamed down my face. I cried so much that my chest began to heave, and then, as if my heaving chest caused her to have some pity on me, she stopped pinching and began to kiss me on the same spots where shortly before I had felt the pain of her pinch. Oh, the sensation was delicious—the combination of pinches and kisses. And so wonderful we found it that, almost every time we met, pinching by her, followed by tears from me, followed by kisses from her were the order of the day. I stopped wondering why all the girls whom I had mistreated and abandoned followed me around with looks of love and adoration on their faces.

I now quite regularly had to observe a field or something for drawing class; collect specimens of leaves, flowers, or whole plants for botany class; gather specimens of rocks for geography class. In other words, my untruthfulness apparatus was now in full gear. My mother, keeping the usual close tabs, marveled at my industriousness and ambition. I was already first in my class, and I was first without ever really trying hard, so I had nothing much to worry about. I was such a good liar that, almost as if to prove all too true my mother's saying "Where there's a liar, there's a thief," I began to steal. But how could

I not? I had no money of my own. And what a pleasure it was to bring a gift and see that red face, on receiving it, grow even redder in the light of the setting sun on the balcony at the top of the lighthouse. Reaching into my mother's purse for the odd penny or so was easy enough to do, I had had some practice at it. But that wasn't enough to buy two yards of multicolored grosgrain ribbon, or a pair of ring combs studded with rhinestones, or a pair of artificial rosebuds suitable for wearing at the waist of a nice dress. I hardly asked myself what use the Red Girl could really have for these gifts; I hardly cared that she only glanced at them for a moment and then placed them in a pocket of her dirty dress. I simply loved giving her things. But where did I get the money for them? I knew where my parents stored a key to a safe in which they kept what was to me a lot of money. It wasn't long before I could get the key, unlock the safe, and remove some money, and I am sure I could have done this blindfolded. If they missed it, they must have chalked it up to a mistake. It was a pleasure to see that they didn't know everything.

One afternoon, after making some outlandish claim of devotion to my work at school, I told my mother that I was going off to observe or collect—it was all the same to me—one ridiculous thing or other. I was off to see the Red Girl, of course, and I was especially happy to be going on that day because my gift was an unusually beautiful marble—a marble of blue porcelain. I had never seen a marble like it before, and from the time I first saw it I wanted very much to possess it. I had played against the girl to whom it belonged for three days in a row until finally I won all her marbles—thirty-three—except for that one. Then I had to play her and win six games in a row to get the prize—the marble made of blue porcelain. Using the usual slamming-the-gate-and-quietly-creeping-back technique, I dived under the house to retrieve the marble from the special place where I had hidden it. As I came out from under the house, what should I see before me but my mother's two enormous, canvas-clad feet. From the look on my face, she guessed immediately that I was up to something; from the look on her face, I guessed immediately that everything was over. "What do you have in your hand?" she asked, and I had no choice but to open my hand, revealing the hard-earned prize to her angrier and angrier eyes.

My mother said, "Marbles? I had heard you played marbles, but I just couldn't believe it. You were not off to look for plants at all, you were off to play marbles."

"Oh, no," I said. "Oh, no."

"Where are your other marbles?" said my mother. "If you have one, you have many."

"Oh, no," I said. "Oh, no. I don't have marbles, because I don't play marbles."

"You keep them under the house," said my mother, completely ignoring everything I said.

"Oh, no."

"I am going to find them and throw them into the deep sea," she said.

My mother now crawled under the house and began a furious and incredible search for my marbles. If she and I had been taking a walk in the Amazon forest, two of my steps equaling one of her strides, and after a while she noticed that I was no longer at her side, her search for me then would have equaled her search for my marbles now. On and on went her search—behind some planks my father had stored years ago for some long-forgotten use; behind some hatboxes that held old Christmas and birthday cards and old letters from my mother's family; tearing apart my neat pile of books, which, if she had opened any one of them, would have revealed to her, stamped on the title page, these words: "Public Library, Antigua." Of course, that would have been a whole other story, and I can't say which would have been worse, the stolen books or playing marbles. On it went.

"Where are the marbles?" she asked.

"I don't have any marbles," I would reply. "Only this one I found one day as I was crossing the street to school."

Of course I thought, At any minute I am going to die. For there were the marbles staring right at me, staring right at her. Sometimes her hand was actually resting on them. I had stored them in old cans, though my most valued ones were in an old red leather handbag of hers. There they were at her feet, as she rested for a moment, her heel actually digging into the handbag. My heart could have stopped.

My father came home. My mother postponed the rest of the search. Over supper, which, in spite of everything, I was allowed to eat with them, she told him about the marbles, adding a list of things that seemed as long as two chapters from the Old Testament. I could hardly recognize myself from this list— how horrible I was—though all of it was true. But still. They talked about me as if I weren't there sitting in front of them, as if I had boarded a boat for South America without so much as a goodbye. I couldn't remember my mother's being so angry with me ever before; in the meantime all thoughts of the Red Girl vanished from my mind. Trying then to swallow a piece of bread that I had first softened in my gravy, I thought, Well, that's the end of that; if tomorrow I saw that girl on the street, I would just act as if we had never met before, as if her very presence at any time was only an annoyance. As my mother went on to my father in her angry vein, I rearranged my life: Thank God I hadn't abandoned Gwen completely, thank God I was so good at rounders that the girls would be glad to have me head a side again, thank God my breasts hadn't grown and I still needed some tips about them.

Days went by. My mother kept up the search for the marbles. How she would torment me! When

I left for school, she saw me out the gate, then watched me until I was a pin on the horizon. When I came home, there she was, waiting for me. Of course, there was no longer any question of going off in the late afternoon for observations and gatherings. Not that I wanted to anyway—all that was finished. But on it would go. She would ask me for the marbles, and in my sweetest voice I would say I didn't have any. Each of us must have secretly vowed to herself not to give in to the other. But then she tried this new tack. She told me this: When she was a girl, it was her duty to accompany her father up to ground on Saturdays. When they got there, her father would check on the plantain and banana trees, the grapefruit and lime and lemon trees, and check the mongoose traps. Before returning, they would harvest some food for the family to eat in the coming week: plantains, green figs, grapefruit, limes, lemons, coffee beans, cocoa beans, almonds, nutmegs, cloves, dasheen, cassavas, all depending on what was ripe to be harvested. On one particular day, after they had loaded up the donkeys with the provisions, there was an extra bunch of green figs, and my mother was to carry it on her head. She and her father started off for their home, and as they walked my mother noticed that the bunch of figs grew heavier and heavier— much heavier than any bunch of figs she had ever carried before. She ached, from the top of her neck to the base of her spine. The weight of the green figs caused her to walk slowly, and sometimes she lost sight of her father. She was alone on the road, and she heard all sorts of sounds that she had never heard before and sounds that she could not account for. Full of fright and in pain, she walked into her yard, very glad to get rid of the green figs. She no sooner had taken the load from her head when out of it crawled a very long black snake. She didn't have time to shout, it crawled away so quickly into the bushes. Perhaps from fright, perhaps from the weight of the load she had just gotten rid of, she collapsed.

When my mother came to the end of this story, I thought my heart would break. Here was my mother, a girl then, certainly no older than I, traveling up that road from the ground to her house with a snake on her head. I had seen pictures of her at that age. What a beautiful girl she was! So tall and thin. Long, thick black hair, which she wore in two plaits that hung down past her shoulders. Her back was already curved from not ever standing up straight, even though she got repeated warnings. She was so shy that she never smiled enough for you to see her teeth, and if she ever burst out laughing she would instantly cover her mouth with her hands. She always obeyed her mother, and her sister worshipped her. She, in turn, worshipped her brother, John, and when he died of something the doctor knew nothing about, of something the obeah woman knew everything about, my mother refused food for a week. Oh, to think of a dangerous, horrible black snake on top of that beautiful head; to think of those beautifully arched, pink-soled feet (the feet of which mine were an exact replica, as hers were an exact replica of her mother's) stumbling on the stony, uneven road, the weight of snake and green figs too much for that small back. If only I had been there, I would not have hesitated for even a part of a second to take her place. How I would have loved my mother if I had known her then. To have been the same age as someone so beautiful, someone who even then loved books, someone who threw stones at monkeys in the forest! What I wouldn't have done for her. Nothing would ever be too much. And so, feeling such love and such pity for this girl standing in front of me, I was on the verge of giving to my mother my entire collection of marbles. She wanted them so badly. What could some marbles matter? A snake had sat on her head for miles as she walked home. The words "The marbles are in the corner over there" were on the very tip of my tongue, when I heard my mother, her voice warm and soft and treacherous, say to me, "Well, Little Miss, where are your marbles?" Summoning my own warm, soft, and newly acquired treacherous voice, I said, "I don't have any marbles. I have never played marbles, you know."

Soon after, I started to menstruate, and I stopped playing marbles. I never saw the Red Girl again. For a reason not having to do with me, she had been sent to Anguilla to live with her grandparents and finish her schooling. The night of the day I heard about it, I dreamed of her. I dreamed that the boat on which she had been traveling suddenly splintered in the middle of the sea, causing all the passengers to

drown except for her, whom I rescued in a small boat.
I took her to an island, where we lived together forever, I suppose, and fed on wild pigs and sea grapes.
At night, we would sit on the sand and watch ships
filled with people on a cruise steam by. We sent con-
fusing signals to the ships, causing them to crash on
some nearby rocks. How we laughed as their cries of
joy turned to cries of sorrow.

Chapter Five

Columbus in Chains

Outside, as usual, the sun shone, the trade winds blew; on her way to put some starched clothes on the line, my mother shooed some hens out of her garden; Miss Dewberry baked the buns, some of which my mother would buy for my father and me to eat with our afternoon tea; Miss Henry brought the milk, a glass of which I would drink with my lunch, and another glass of which I would drink with the bun from Miss Dewberry; my mother prepared our lunch; my father noted some perfectly idiotic thing his partner in housebuilding, Mr. Oatie, had done, so that over lunch he and my mother could have a good laugh.

The Anglican church bell struck eleven o'clock— one hour to go before lunch. I was then sitting at my desk in my classroom. We were having a history lesson—the last lesson of the morning. For taking first place over all the other girls, I had been given a prize, a copy of a book called *Roman Britain*, and I was made prefect of my class. What a mistake the prefect part had been, for I was among the worst-behaved in my class and did not at all believe in setting myself up as a good example, the way a prefect was supposed to do. Now I had to sit in the prefect's seat—the first seat in the front row, the seat from which I could stand up and survey quite easily my classmates. From where I sat I could see out the window. Sometimes when I looked out, I could see the sexton going over to the minister's house. The sexton's daughter, Hilarene, a disgusting model of good behavior and keen attention to scholarship, sat next to me, since she took second place. The minister's daughter, Ruth, sat in the last row, the row reserved for all the dunce girls. Hilarene, of course, I could not stand. A girl that good would never do for me. I would probably not have cared so much for first place if I could be sure it would not go to her. Ruth I liked, because she was such a dunce and came from England and had yellow hair. When I first met her, I used to walk her home and sing bad songs to her just to see her turn pink, as if I had spilled hot water all over her.

Our books, *A History of the West Indies*, were open in front of us. Our day had begun with morning prayers, then a geometry lesson, then it was over to the science building for a lesson in "Introductory Physics" (not a subject we cared much for), taught by the most dingy-toothed Mr. Slacks, a teacher from Canada, then precious recess, and now this, our history lesson. Recess had the usual drama: this time, I coaxed Gwen out of her disappointment at not being allowed to join the junior choir. Her father—how many times had I wished he would become a leper and so be banished to a leper colony for the rest of my long and happy life with Gwen—had forbidden it, giving as his reason that she lived too far away from church, where choir rehearsals were conducted, and that it would be dangerous for her, a young girl, to walk home alone at night in the dark. Of course, all the streets had lamplight, but it was useless to point that out to him. Oh, how it would have pleased us to press and rub our knees together as we sat in our pew while pretending to pay close attention to Mr. Simmons, our choirmaster, as he waved his baton up and down and across, and how it would have pleased us even more to walk home together, alone in the "early dusk" (the way Gwen had phrased it, a ready phrase always on her tongue), stopping, if there was a full moon, to lie down in a pasture and expose our bosoms in the moonlight. We had heard that full moonlight would make our breasts grow to a size we would like. Poor Gwen! When I first heard from her that she was one of ten children, right on the spot I told her that I would love only her, since her mother already had so many other people to love.

Our teacher, Miss Edward, paced up and down in front of the class in her usual way. In front of her desk stood a small table, and on it stood the dunce cap. The dunce cap was in the shape of a coronet, with an adjustable opening in the back, so that it could fit any head. It was made of cardboard with a shiny gold paper covering and the word "DUNCE" in shiny red paper on the front. When the sun shone on it, the dunce cap was all aglitter, almost as if you were being tricked into thinking it a desirable thing to wear. As Miss Edward paced up and down, she would pass between us and the dunce cap like an eclipse. Each Friday morning, we were given a small test to see how well we had learned the things taught to us all week. The girl who scored lowest was made to wear the dunce cap all day the following Monday. On many Mondays, Ruth wore it—only, with her short yellow hair, when the dunce cap was sitting on her head she looked like a girl attending a birthday party in *The Schoolgirl's Own Annual.*

It was Miss Edward's way to ask one of us a question the answer to which she was sure the girl would not know and then put the same question to another girl who she was sure would know the answer. The girl who did not answer correctly would then have to repeat the correct answer in the exact words of the other girl. Many times, I had heard my exact words repeated over and over again, and I liked it especially when the girl doing the repeating was one I didn't care about very much. Pointing a finger at Ruth, Miss Edward asked a question the answer to which was "On the third of November 1493, a Sunday morning, Christopher Columbus discovered Dominica." Ruth, of course, did not know the answer, as she did not know the answer to many questions about the West Indies. I could hardly blame her. Ruth had come all the way from England. Perhaps she did not want to be in the West Indies at all. Perhaps she wanted to be in England, where no one would remind her constantly of the terrible things her ancestors had done; perhaps she had felt even worse when her father was a missionary in Africa. I could see how Ruth felt from looking at her face. Her ancestors had been the masters, while ours had been the slaves. She had such a lot to be ashamed of, and by being with us every day she was always being reminded. We could look everybody in the eye, for our ancestors had done nothing wrong except just sit somewhere, defenseless. Of course, sometimes, what with our teachers and our books, it was hard for us to tell on which side we really now belonged—with the masters or the slaves—for it was all history, it was all in the past, and everybody behaved differently now; all of us celebrated Queen Victoria's birthday, even though she had been dead a long time. But we, the descendants of the slaves, knew quite well what had really happened, and I was sure that if the tables had been turned we would have acted differently; I was sure that if our ancestors had gone from Africa to Europe and come upon the people living there, they would have taken a proper interest in the Europeans on first seeing them, and said, "How nice," and then gone home to tell their friends about it.

I was sitting at my desk, having these thoughts to myself. I don't know how long it had been since I

lost track of what was going on around me. I had
not noticed that the girl who was asked the question
after Ruth failed—a girl named Hyacinth—had only
got a part of the answer correct. I had not noticed
that after these two attempts Miss Edward had
launched into a harangue about what a worthless
bunch we were compared to girls of the past. In fact,
I was no longer on the same chapter we were studying. I was way ahead, at the end of the chapter about
Columbus's third voyage. In this chapter, there was
a picture of Columbus that took up a whole page, and
it was in color—one of only five color pictures in the
book. In this picture, Columbus was seated in the
bottom of a ship. He was wearing the usual three-
quarter trousers and a shirt with enormous sleeves,
both the trousers and shirt made of maroon-colored
velvet. His hat, which was cocked up on one side of
his head, had a gold feather in it, and his black shoes
had huge gold buckles. His hands and feet were
bound up in chains, and he was sitting there staring
off into space, looking quite dejected and miserable.
The picture had as a title "Columbus in Chains,"
printed at the bottom of the page. What had happened was that the usually quarrelsome Columbus
had got into a disagreement with people who were
even more quarrelsome, and a man named Bobadilla,
representing King Ferdinand and Queen Isabella,
had sent him back to Spain fettered in chains at-
tached to the bottom of a ship. What just deserts, I
thought, for I did not like Columbus. How I loved
this picture—to see the usually triumphant Colum-

bus, brought so low, seated at the bottom of a boat just watching things go by. Shortly after I first discovered it in my history book, I heard my mother read out loud to my father a letter she had received from her sister, who still lived with her mother and father in the very same Dominica, which is where my mother came from. Ma Chess was fine, wrote my aunt, but Pa Chess was not well. Pa Chess was having a bit of trouble with his limbs; he was not able to go about as he pleased; often he had to depend on someone else to do one thing or another for him. My mother read the letter in quite a state, her voice rising to a higher pitch with each sentence. After she read the part about Pa Chess's stiff limbs, she turned to my father and laughed as she said, "So the great man can no longer just get up and go. How I would love to see his face now!" When I next saw the picture of Columbus sitting there all locked up in his chains, I wrote under it the words "The Great Man Can No Longer Just Get Up and Go." I had written this out with my fountain pen, and in Old English lettering— a script I had recently mastered. As I sat there looking at the picture, I traced the words with my pen over and over, so that the letters grew big and you could read what I had written from not very far away. I don't know how long it was before I heard that my name, Annie John, was being said by this bellowing dragon in the form of Miss Edward bearing down on me.

I had never been a favorite of hers. Her favorite was Hilarene. It must have pained Miss Edward that I so often beat out Hilarene. Not that I liked Miss

Edward and wanted her to like me back, but all my other teachers regarded me with much affection, would always tell my mother that I was the most charming student they had ever had, beamed at me when they saw me coming, and were very sorry when they had to write some version of this on my report card: "Annie is an unusually bright girl. She is well behaved in class, at least in the presence of her masters and mistresses, but behind their backs and outside the classroom quite the opposite is true." When my mother read this or something like it, she would burst into tears. She had hoped to display, with a great flourish, my report card to her friends, along with whatever prize I had won. Instead, the report card would have to take a place at the bottom of the old trunk in which she kept any important thing that had to do with me. I became not a favorite of Miss Edward's in the following way: Each Friday afternoon, the girls in the lower forms were given, instead of a last lesson period, an extra-long recess. We were to use this in ladylike recreation—walks, chats about the novels and poems we were reading, showing each other the new embroidery stitches we had learned to master in home class, or something just as seemly. Instead, some of the girls would play a game of cricket or rounders or stones, but most of us would go to the far end of the school grounds and play band. In this game, of which teachers and parents disapproved and which was sometimes absolutely forbidden, we would place our arms around each other's waist or shoulders, forming lines of ten or so girls, and then we would dance from one end of the school grounds to the other. As we danced, we would sometimes chant these words: "Tee la la la, come go. Tee la la la, come go." At other times we would sing a popular calypso song which usually had lots of unladylike words to it. Up and down the schoolyard, away from our teachers, we would dance and sing. At the end of recess—forty-five minutes—we were missing ribbons and other ornaments from our hair, the pleats of our linen tunics became unset, the collars of our blouses were pulled out, and we were soaking wet all the way down to our bloomers. When the school bell rang, we would make a whooping sound, as if in a great panic, and then we would throw ourselves on top of each other as we laughed and shrieked. We would then run back to our classes, where we prepared to file into the auditorium for evening prayers. After that, it was home for the weekend. But how could we go straight home after all that excitement? No sooner were we on the street than we would form little groups, depending on the direction we were headed in. I was never keen on joining them on the way home, because I was sure I would run into my mother. Instead, my friends and I would go to our usual place near the back of the churchyard and sit on the tombstones of people who had been buried there way before slavery was abolished, in 1833. We would sit and sing bad songs, use forbidden words, and, of course, show each other various parts of our bodies. While some of us watched, the others would walk up and down on the large tombstones showing off their legs. It was immediately a popular idea; everybody soon wanted to do it. It wasn't long before many girls—the ones whose mothers didn't pay strict attention to what they were doing—started to come to school on Fridays wearing not bloomers under their uniforms but underpants trimmed with lace and satin frills. It also wasn't long before an end came to all that. One Friday afternoon, Miss Edward, on her way home from school, took a shortcut through the churchyard. She must have heard the commotion we were making, because there she suddenly was, saying, "What is the meaning of this?"—just the very thing someone like her would say if she came unexpectedly on something like us. It was obvious that I was the ringleader. Oh, how I wished the ground would open up and take her in, but it did not. We all, shamefacedly, slunk home, I with Miss Edward at my side. Tears came to my mother's eyes when she heard what I had done. It was apparently such a bad thing that my mother couldn't bring herself to repeat my misdeed to my father in my presence. I got the usual punishment of dinner alone, outside under the breadfruit tree, but added on to that, I was not allowed to go to the library on Saturday, and on Sunday, after Sunday school and dinner, I was not allowed to take a stroll in the botanical gardens, where Gwen was waiting for me in the bamboo grove.

That happened when I was in the first form. Now here Miss Edward stood. Her whole face was on fire. Her eyes were bulging out of her head. I was sure that at any minute they would land at my feet and roll away. The small pimples on her face, already looking as if they were constantly irritated, now ballooned into huge, on-the-verge-of-exploding boils. Her head shook from side to side. Her strange bottom, which she carried high in the air, seemed to rise up so high that it almost touched the ceiling. Why did I not pay attention, she said. My impertinence was beyond endurance. She then found a hundred words for the different forms my impertinence took. On she went. I was just getting used to this amazing bellowing when suddenly she was speechless. In fact, everything stopped. Her eyes stopped, her bottom stopped, her pimples stopped. Yes, she had got close enough so that her eyes caught a glimpse of what I had done to my textbook. The glimpse soon led to closer inspection. It was bad enough that I had defaced my schoolbook by writing in it. That I should write under the picture of Columbus "The Great Man . . ." etc. was just too much. I had gone too far this time, defaming one of the great men in history, Christopher Columbus, discoverer of the island that was my home. And now look at me. I was not even hanging my head in remorse. Had my peers ever seen anyone so arrogant, so blasphemous?

I was sent to the headmistress, Miss Moore. As punishment, I was removed from my position as prefect, and my place was taken by the odious Hilarene. As an added punishment, I was ordered to copy Books I and II of *Paradise Lost*, by John Milton, and to have it done a week from that day. I then couldn't

wait to get home to lunch and the comfort of my
mother's kisses and arms. I had nothing to worry about
there yet; it would be a while before my mother and
father heard of my bad deeds. What a terrible morning! Seeing my mother would be such a tonic—something to pick me up.

When I got home, my mother kissed me absent-
mindedly. My father had got home ahead of me, and
they were already deep in conversation, my father
regaling her with some unusually outlandish thing
the oaf Mr. Oatie had done. I washed my hands and
took my place at table. My mother brought me my
lunch. I took one smell of it, and I could tell that it
was the much hated breadfruit. My mother said not at
all, it was a new kind of rice imported from Belgium,
and not breadfruit, mashed and forced through a
ricer, as I thought. She went back to talking to my
father. My father could hardly get a few words out of
his mouth before she was a jellyfish of laughter. I sat
there, putting my food in my mouth. I could not
believe that she couldn't see how miserable I was
and so reach out a hand to comfort me and caress
my cheek, the way she usually did when she sensed
that something was amiss with me. I could not believe how she laughed at everything he said, and how
bitter it made me feel to see how much she liked
him. I ate my meal. The more I ate of it, the more
I was sure that it was breadfruit. When I finished,
my mother got up to remove my plate. As she started
out the door, I said, "Tell me, really, the name of the
thing I just ate."

My mother said, "You just ate some breadfruit. I made it look like rice so that you would eat it. It's very good for you, filled with lots of vitamins." As she said this, she laughed. She was standing half inside the door, half outside. Her body was in the shade of our house, but her head was in the sun. When she laughed, her mouth opened to show off big, shiny, sharp white teeth. It was as if my mother had suddenly turned into a crocodile.

Chapter Six

Somewhere, Belgium

In the year I turned fifteen, I felt more un-
happy than I had ever imagined anyone could be. It
wasn't the unhappiness of wanting a new dress, or the
unhappiness of wanting to go to cinema on a Sunday
afternoon and not being allowed to do so, or the unhappiness of being unable to solve some mystery in
geometry, or the unhappiness at causing my dearest
friend, Gwen, some pain. My unhappiness was something deep inside me, and when I closed my eyes I
could even see it. It sat somewhere—maybe in my
belly, maybe in my heart; I could not exactly tell—
and it took the shape of a small black ball, all wrapped
up in cobwebs. I would look at it and look at it until
I had burned the cobwebs away, and then I would see
that the ball was no bigger than a thimble, even
though it weighed worlds. At that moment, just
when I saw its size and felt its weight, I was beyond

feeling sorry for myself, which is to say I was beyond tears. I could only just sit and look at myself, feeling like the oldest person who had ever lived and who had not learned a single thing. After I had sat in this way for a while, to distract myself I would count my toes; always it came out the same—I had ten of them.

If I had been asked, I would not have been able to say exactly how it was that I got that way. It must have come on me like mist: first, I was in just a little mist and could still see everything around me, though not so clearly; then I was completely covered up and could not see even my own hand stretched out in front of me. I tried to imagine that I was like a girl in one of the books I had read—a girl who had suffered much at the hands of a cruel step-parent, or a girl who suddenly found herself without any parents at all. When reading about such a girl, I would heap even more suffering on her if I felt the author hadn't gone far enough. In the end, of course, everything was resolved happily for the girl, and she and a companion would sail off to Zanzibar or some other very distant place, where, since they could do as they pleased, they were forever happy. But I was not in a book. I was always just sitting there with the thimble that weighed worlds fastened deep inside me, the sun beating down on me. Everything I used to care about had turned sour. I could start with the sight of the flamboyant trees in bloom, the red of the flowers causing the street on which I lived to seem on fire at sunset; seeing this sight, I would imagine myself in-

capable of coming to harm if I were just to walk
through this inferno. I could end with my mother
and me; we were now a sight to see.

We both noticed that now if she said that something I did reminded her of her own self at my age,
I would try to do it a different way, or, failing that,
do it in a way that she could not stomach. She returned the blow by admiring and praising everything
that she suspected had special meaning for me. I
became secretive, and she said that I was in practice
for becoming a liar and a thief—the only kinds of
people who had secrets. My mother and I each soon
grew two faces: one for my father and the rest of the
world, and one for us when we found ourselves alone
with each other. For my father and the world, we
were politeness and kindness and love and laughter.
I saw her with my old eyes, my eyes as a child, and
she saw me with hers of that time. There was my
mother scrubbing my back as in the old days, examin-
ing my body from limb to limb, making sure nothing
unusual was taking place; there was my mother making me my favorite dessert, a blancmange—a reward
for excelling at something that met her approval;
there was my mother concerned about a small sniffle,
wondering if soon it would develop into something
major and then she would have to make me a poultice
of ground camphor and eucalyptus leaves for my
chest. And there I was also, letting the singsong of
her voice, as it expressed love and concern, calm me
into a lull; there I was fondling the strands of her
thick black hair as she unraveled her braids for a

daily brushing, burying my face in it and inhaling deeply, for it smelled of rose oil.

As we were playing out these scenes from the old days, the house would swell with the sound of my father's voice telling one story after another of his days as a famous batsman with a cricket team, and of what he did on this island and the next as he toured the Windward and the Leeward Islands with his teammates. In front of my mother's friends also, we put on our good faces. I was obedient and nice, and she asked nothing more than that I show the good manners she had taught me. Sometimes on Sundays as we walked back from church, perhaps touched by the sermon we had just heard, we would link arms as we strolled home, step in step with each other.

But no sooner were we alone, behind the fence, behind the closed door, than everything darkened. How to account for it I could not say. Something I could not name just came over us, and suddenly I had never loved anyone so or hated anyone so. But to say hate—what did I mean by that? Before, if I hated someone I simply wished the person dead. But I couldn't wish my mother dead. If my mother died, what would become of me? I couldn't imagine my life without her. Worse than that, if my mother died I would have to die, too, and even less than I could imagine my mother dead could I imagine myself dead.

I started to have a dream. In my dream, I walked down a smooth, unpaved road. The road was lined on either side with palm trees whose leaves spread out so wide that they met and tangled up with each other and the whole road was shaded from the sun, which was always shining. When I started to walk down the road, my steps were quick and light, and as I walked these words would go around in my head: "My mother would kill me if she got the chance. I would kill my mother if I had the courage." At the beginning of my walk, as I chanted the words my voice had a happy note, as if the quickness and lightness of my feet signaled to me that I would never give her the chance. But as the road went on, things changed. I would say the same words, but slower and slower and in a sad way; my feet and the rest of my body became heavy. It was as if it had dawned on me that I would never have the courage with which to kill my mother, and then, since I lacked the courage, the chance would pass to her. I did not understand how it became so, but just the same it did. I had been taught by my mother to take my dreams seriously. My dreams were not unreal representations of something real; my dreams were a part of, and the same as, my real life. When I first had this dream, I became quite frightened of my mother, and I was so ashamed of it that I couldn't bring myself to look directly at her. But after I had had the dream again and again, it became like a second view to me, and I would hold up little incidents against it to see if this was her chance or that was my courage.

At school, I had had a great change. I was no longer in the same class with Gwen; I was now in a class with girls two or three years older than I was. That was a shock. These girls didn't offer the camaraderie of my friends in the second form. They didn't have the give-and-take, the friendly pull-and-shove. They were constantly in strict competition for good marks and our teachers' affection, and among them insults ruled the day. And how vain they were! Constantly they smoothed down their hair, making sure every strand was in place; some carried mirrors in their schoolbags, and they would hold them at an angle to see if the pleats in the backs of their uniforms were in place. They actually practiced walking with their hips swinging from side to side. They were always sticking out their bosoms, and, what was worse, they actually did have bosoms to stick out. Before I got to see these girls close up—when I was just observing them as they walked to and fro, going about their business—I envied the way the air seemed to part for them, freeing itself of any obstacle so that they wouldn't have to make an effort. Now I could see that the air just parted itself quickly so that it wouldn't have to bear their company for long. For what a dull bunch they were! They had no different ideas of how to be in the world; they certainly didn't think that the world was a strange place to be caught living in.

I was at first slowed down in my usual climb to the top by the new subjects put before me, but I soon mastered them, and only one other girl was my match. Sometimes we tied for first place, sometimes she was first and I second, and sometimes it was the other way around. I tried to get to know her, feeling that we had this much in common, but she was so dull a person, completely unable to hold so much as a simple conversation, and, to boot, smelled so of old rubber and blue ink, that I made myself unable to remember her name. I could see the kind of grownup person she would be—just the kind who would take one look at me and put every effort into making my life a hardship. Already her mouth was turned down permanently at the corners, as if to show that she had been born realizing that nobody else behaved properly, and as if also she had been born knowing that everything in life was a disappointment and her face was all set to meet it.

Gwen and I walked home from school in the usual way and did the usual things, but just the sight of her was no longer a thrill to me, though I did my best not to let her know. It was as if I had grown a new skin over the old skin and the new skin had a completely different set of nerve endings. But what could I say to poor Gwen? How to explain to her about the thimble that weighed worlds, and the dark cloud that was like an envelope in which my mother and I were sealed? If I said to Gwen, "Does your mother always watch you out of the corner of her eye?" her reply was most likely to be "My mother has a knack for keeping her eye on everything at the same time." And if I said, "I don't mean in that way, I mean—" But what would have been the use of going on? We no longer lived on the same plane. Sometimes, just hearing her voice as she ran on and on, bringing me up to date on the doings of my old group, would put me in such a state that I felt I would explode; and then I remembered that it was the same voice that used to be, for me, some sort of music. How small she now looked in my eyes: a bundle of who said what and who did what.

One day when we were walking home, taking the lane with the big houses hidden behind the high hedges, Gwen said to me that her brother Rowan had mentioned how much he liked the way I had conducted myself when I was asked to read the lesson in church one Sunday. She then launched into a long speech about him, and I did what was fast becoming a habit when we were together: I started to daydream. My most frequent daydream now involved scenes of me living alone in Belgium, a place I had picked when I read in one of my books that Charlotte Brontë, the author of my favorite novel, *Jane Eyre*, had spent a year or so there. I had also picked it because I imagined that it would be a place my mother would find difficult to travel to and so would have to write me letters addressed in this way:

> *To: Miss Annie Victoria John*
> *Somewhere,*
> *Belgium*

I was walking down a street in Belgium, wearing a skirt that came down to my ankles and carrying a bag filled with books that at last I could understand, when suddenly I heard these words come out of Gwen's mouth: "I think it would be so nice if you married Rowan. Then, you see, that way we could be together always."

I was brought back to the present, and I stopped and stood still for a moment; then my mouth fell open and my whole self started to tremble. All this was in disbelief, of course, but, to show how far apart we were, she thought that my mouth fell open and my whole self trembled in complete joy at what she had said to me. And when I said, "What did you just say?" she said, "Oh, I knew you would like the idea." I felt so alone; the last person left on earth couldn't feel more alone than I. I looked at Gwen. Could this really be Gwen? It was Gwen. The same person I had always known. Everything was in place. But at the same time something terrible had happened, and I couldn't tell what it was.

It was then that I began avoiding Gwen and our daily walks home. I tried not to do it so much that she would notice, but about every three or four days I would say that being in my new class was so demanding and, what with one thing and another, I had things to clear up here and there. I would walk her to the school gate, where we would kiss goodbye, and then, after some proper time had passed, I would leave school. One afternoon, I took another way home, a way that brought me through Market Street. Market Street was where all the stores were, and I passed by slowly, staring into the shop windows, though I wasn't at all interested in the merchandise on display. What I was really looking at was my own reflection in the glass, though it was a while before I knew that. I saw myself just hanging there among bolts of cloth, among Sunday hats and shoes, among men's and women's undergarments, among pots and pans, among brooms and household soap, among notebooks and pens and ink, among medicines for curing headache and medicines for curing colds. I saw myself among all these things, but I didn't know that it was I, for I had got so strange. My whole head was so big, and my eyes, which were big, too, sat in my big head wide open, as if I had just had a sudden fright. My skin was black in a way I had not noticed before, as if someone had thrown a lot of soot out of a window just when I was passing by and it had all fallen on me. On my forehead, on my cheeks were little bumps, each with a perfect, round white point. My plaits stuck out in every direction from under my hat; my long, thin neck stuck out from the blouse of my uniform. Altogether, I looked old and miserable. Not long before, I had seen a picture of a painting entitled *The Young Lucifer*. It showed Satan just recently cast out of heaven for all his bad deeds, and he was standing on a black rock all alone and naked. Everything around him was charred and black, as if a great fire had just roared through. His skin was coarse, and so were all his features. His hair was made up of live snakes, and they were in a position to strike. Satan was wearing a smile, but it was one of those smiles that you could see through, one of those smiles that make you know the person is just putting up a good front. At heart, you could see, he was really lonely and miserable at the way things had turned out. I was standing there surprised at this change in myself, when all this came to mind, and suddenly I felt so sorry for myself that I was about to sit down on the sidewalk and weep, already tasting the salty bitterness of my tears.

I was about to do this when I noticed four boys standing across the street from me; they were looking at me and bowing as they said, in an exaggerated tone of voice, pretending to be grownup gentlemen living in Victorian times, "Hallo, Madame. How are you this afternoon?" and "What a pleasant thing, our running into each other like this," and "We meet again after all this time," and "Ah, the sun, it shines and shines only on you." The words were no sooner out of their mouths than they would bend over laughing. Even though nothing like this had ever happened to me before, I knew instantly that it was malicious and that I had done nothing to deserve it other than standing there all alone. They were older than I, and from their uniforms I could tell that they were students of the boys' branch of my own school. I looked at their faces. I didn't recognize the first, I didn't recognize the second, I didn't recognize the third, but I knew the face of the fourth one; it was a face from my ancient history. A long time ago, when we were little children, our mothers were best friends, and he and I used to play together. His name was Mineu, and I felt pleased that he, a boy older than I by three years, would play with me. Of course, in all the games we played I was always given the lesser part. If we played knight and dragon, I was the dragon; if we played discovering Africa, he discovered Africa; he was also the leader of the savage tribes that tried to get in the way of the discovery, and I played his servant, and a not very bright servant at that; if we played prodigal son, he was the prodigal son and the prodigal son's father and the jealous brother, while I played a person who fetched things.

Once, in a game we were playing, something terrible happened. A man had recently killed his girlfriend and a man who was his best friend when he found them drinking together in a bar. Their blood splattered all over him. The cutlass he had used to kill them in hand, he walked the mile or so to the police station with the other customers of the bar and some people they picked up along the way. The murder of these two people immediately became a big scandal, and the most popular calypso song that year was all about it. It became a big scandal because the murderer was from an old, well-off, respected family, and everybody wondered if he would be hanged, which was the penalty for murder; also it became a scandal because everyone had known the woman and all had predicted that she would come to a bad end. Everything about this soon became a spectacle. During the funerals of the murdered man and woman, people lined the streets and followed the hearses from the church to the cemetery. During the trial of the murderer, the courtroom was always packed. When the judge sentenced the man to be hanged, the whole courtroom gasped in shock. On the morning that he was hanged, people gathered outside the jail and waited until the jail's church bell rang, showing that the hanging was completed. Mineu and I had overheard our parents talk so much about this event that it wasn't long before he made up a game about it. As usual, Mineu played all the big parts. He played the murdered man and the murderer, going back and forth; the girlfriend we left silent. When the case got to court, Mineu played judge, jury, prosecutor, and condemned man, sitting in the condemned man's box. Nothing was funnier than seeing him, using some old rags as a wig for his part of the judge, pass sentence on himself; nothing was funnier than seeing him, as the drunken hangman, hang himself. And after he was hanged, I, as his mother, came and wept over the body as it lay on the ground. Then we would get up and start the whole thing over again. No sooner had we completed the episode than we were back at the bar, with Mineu quarreling with himself and his girlfriend and then putting an end to everything with a few quick strokes. We always tried to make every detail as close to the real thing as we imagined it, and so we had gone to the trouble of finding old furniture to make a desk for the judge and a place for the jury to sit, and we set out some stones facing the judge to represent both where the spectators might sit and the spectators themselves. When it came to the hanging, we wanted that to be real, too, so Mineu had found a piece of rope and tied it to the top bar of the gate to his yard, and then he would make a noose and put his head in it. When the noose was around his neck, he would grab the rope from above and then swing on it back and forth to show that he was hanged and already dead. All of our playing together came to an end when something bad almost happened. We were playing in the usual way when we came to the part of the noose around the neck. When he lifted himself off the ground, the noose tightened. When he let go of the rope to loosen the noose with his hands, that only made matters worse, and the noose tightened even more. His mouth opened as he tried to get breath, and then his tongue began to come out of his mouth. His body, hanging from the gate, began to swing back and forth, and as it did it banged against the gate, and it made a sound as if he were swinging on the gate—the very thing we were always being told not to do. As all this happened, I just stood there and stared. I must have known that I should go and call for help, but I was unable to move. *Slam, slam* went the gate, and soon his mother began to call out, "Children, leave the gate alone." Then, hearing the gate continue to slam, she came out to us in a fury, because we were not obeying her, and she was just about to shout at us when she saw her child swinging from the gate by his neck. She screamed and rushed over to him, calling out to a neighbor, who came immediately with a cutlass and cut the rope from around Mineu's neck. When his mother came and

started to scream, only then could I scream, too, and
I ran over to him with her, and we both cried over
him as he fell to the ground. Much was said about
my not calling for help, and everybody wondered
what would have happened if his mother hadn't been
nearby. I didn't know what to make of my own
behavior, and I could not explain myself, as everybody kept asking me to do. I could see that even my
mother was ashamed of the way I had behaved.

It was this that I remembered as I saw Mineu's
face across the street, and so I walked over and said
in my best, most polite young-lady voice, "Hallo,
Mineu. I am so glad to see you. Don't you remember
me?" It was true that I was glad to see him. For just
remembering all the things that he and I used to do
reminded me of how happy I had been and how
much my mother and everyone else adored me and
how, when looking at me, people used to say, "What
a beautiful child!"

At first, he just looked at me. Then he said, "Oh,
yes. Annie. Annie John. I remember you. I had heard
you were a big girl now." As he said this, he shook
my outstretched hand. His friends stood off to one
side, a little bit apart from us. They stood in that
ridiculous way of boys: one leg crossing the other,
hands jammed deep into pockets, eyes looking you
up and down. They were whispering things to each
other, and their shoulders were heaving with amuse-
ment—at me, I could only suppose. I thought that
since he was someone I knew, he couldn't really be
like them, but as we stood, more or less speechless, in

front of each other, I saw him glancing at them out of the corner of his eye, smiling in a knowing way and then looking back straight at me, a serious look on his face.

Feeling ashamed, for I could tell that they were making fun of me, I said to him, "Well, goodbye then," and I offered him my hand again.

He and his friends walked off, their backs shaking with laughter—at me, no doubt. As I watched them, I wished that right there I could turn them into cinder blocks, so that one moment if you were walking behind them you were walking behind four boys and the next moment you had to be careful not to stumble over some cinder blocks. Feeling that in this whole incident Mineu had been cruel made me remember something. It was the last time that we had played together. In a game we were making up on the spot, I took off all my clothes and he led me to a spot under a tree, where I was to sit until he told me what to do next. It wasn't long before I realized that the spot he had picked out was a red ants' nest. Soon the angry ants were all over me, stinging me in my private parts, and as I cried and scratched, trying to get the ants off me, he fell down on the ground laughing, his feet kicking the air with happiness. His mother refused to admit that he had done something wrong, and my mother never spoke to her again.

I walked home, cutting through the church-yard of the Methodist church (my own church). Except for two lizards chasing each other across my path, I wasn't aware of anything on the outside. Inside, however, the thimble that weighed worlds spun around and around; as it spun, it bumped up against my heart, my chest, my stomach, and whatever it touched felt as if I had been scorched there. I thought that I had better get home quickly, for I began to feel alternately too big and too small. First, I grew so big that I took up the whole street; then I grew so small that nobody could see me—not even if I cried out.

I walked into our yard, and I could see my mother standing in the kitchen, her back toward me, bent over a bowl in which she was putting some green figs, their skins removed. I walked up to her and I said, "Good afternoon, Mamie. I have just come home from school."

My mother turned to face me. We looked at each other, and I could see the frightening black thing leave her to meet the frightening black thing that had left me. They met in the middle and embraced. What will it be now, I asked myself. To me she said, "You are late. It would please me to hear an excuse from you." She was using that tone of voice: it was as if I were not only a stranger but a stranger that she did not wish to know.

Trying to match her tone of voice but coming nowhere near success, I said something about being kept late for extra studies. I then went on to say that my teachers believed that if I studied hard enough, by my sixteenth birthday I might be able to take final exams and so be able to leave school.

As if she knew exactly that I would come up with some such story, she said, "Perhaps if I ask again this time I will get a straight answer." I was about to make a feeble effort at protest, but then, in a rush, she said that she had been standing inside a store that afternoon, buying some buttons for a Sunday dress for me, when, on looking up, she observed me making a spectacle of myself in front of four boys. She went on to say that, after all the years she had spent drumming into me the proper way to conduct myself when speaking to young men, it had pained her to see me behave in the manner of a slut (only she used the French-patois word for it) in the street and that just to see me had caused her to feel shame.

The word "slut" (in patois) was repeated over and over, until suddenly I felt as if I were drowning in a well but instead of the well being filled with water it was filled with the word "slut," and it was pouring in through my eyes, my ears, my nostrils, my mouth. As if to save myself, I turned to her and said, "Well, like father like son, like mother like daughter."

At that, everything stopped. The whole earth fell silent. The two black things joined together in the middle of the room separated, hers going to her, mine coming back to me. I looked at my mother. She seemed tired and old and broken. Seeing that, I felt happy and sad at the same time. I soon decided that happy was better, and I was just about to enjoy this feeling when she said, "Until this moment, in my whole life I knew without a doubt that, without any exception, I loved you best," and then she turned her back and started again to prepare the green figs for cooking.

I looked at my mother—at her turned back this time—and she wasn't tired and old and broken at all. She wore her hair pinned up in the same beautiful way, exposing the nape of her beautiful neck; her bent-over back looked strong and soft at the same time, and I wanted to go and rest my whole body on it the way I used to; her long skirt covered her beautiful, strong legs, and she wore shoes that exposed beautiful heels. It was I who was tired and old and broken, and as I looked at my mother, full of vigor, young and whole, I wanted to go over and put my arms around her and beg forgiveness for the thing I had just said and to explain that I didn't really mean it. But I couldn't move, and when I looked down it was as if the ground had opened up between us, making a deep and wide split. On one side of this split stood my mother, bent over my dinner cooking in a pot; on the other side stood I, in my arms carrying my schoolbooks and inside carrying the thimble that weighed worlds.

I went to my room to take off my school uniform, but I could only sit on my bed and wonder what would become of me now. As I sat, I looked at the things surrounding me. There was my washstand, made for me by my father from pitch pine, with its enamel basin on top and matching urn filled with water underneath; there was my bureau, made for me by my father from pitch pine, and in it were my clothes; there was a shelf made for me by my father from pitch pine on which I kept my books; the very bed I sat on was made for me by my father from pitch pine; there was a little desk and chair to match at which I sat and read or did my homework, both made for me by my father from pitch pine. Each time my father had bought the wood for the furniture, he had taken me to the lumber yard with him, and I saw how he examined every piece of wood carefully before he accepted it for purchase. He would hold it first to his nostrils, then to my own, and he would say, "Nothing like a nice piece of pine, except perhaps a nice piece of mahogany." Then I was not allowed to see the furniture in any stage until it was in its place in my room. It would be a surprise then for me to see it, and I would say to my father, "I see I have a new chair," and he would say, "I see you have a new chair," and then we would embrace, I kissing him on the cheek and he kissing me on the forehead. It used to be that when my father wanted to kiss me he would have to bend down to reach my forehead. Now, in the last year, I had grown so much that it was I who had to bend down so that my father could reach my forehead. My mother was taller than my father. Now I, too, was taller than my father. I was, in fact, as tall as my mother. When my mother and I spoke to each other, we looked at each other eye to eye. Eye to eye. It was the first time such a thing had come to me: my mother and I were eye to eye. For a moment, I was happy at the thought, but then I could see: what did such a thing matter? She was my mother, Annie; I was her daughter, Annie; and that was why I was called by my mother and father Little Miss.

Sitting on my bed and thinking in this way, I swung my feet back and forth, and it was a while before I realized that when they swung back my feet would hit up against the trunk stored under my bed. It was the trunk that my mother had bought when she was sixteen years old—a year older than I was now—and in which she had packed all her things and left not only her parents' house in Dominica but Dominica itself for Antigua. Her father and she had had a big quarrel over whether she would live alone, as she wished, or would continue to live in her parents' house, as her father wished. Her mother, who had stopped speaking to her father a long time before, though they continued to live in the same house, didn't say anything one way or the other. My mother and her father had had a big quarrel, and though my mother had never told me in detail the whole story, I had pieced it together from things I had overheard, just putting two and two together in my usual way. Inside this trunk now were the things, all of them, that had been a part of my life at every stage, and if someone had come upon it without having an inkling of what my life had really been like, they would have got a pretty good idea. As my heels bumped up against the trunk, my heart just broke, and I cried and cried. At that moment, I missed my mother more than I had ever imagined possible and wanted only to live somewhere quiet and beautiful with her alone, but also at that moment I wanted only to see her lying dead, all withered and in a coffin at my feet.

The moment soon passed, and I got up from my bed to change my clothes and carry out my afternoon chores. My mother and I avoided each other, and it wasn't until over our supper of the green figs, cooked with fish in coconut milk, that we looked at each other again. We did our best to keep up appearances, for my father's sake, but our two black things got the better of us, and even though we didn't say anything noticeable it was clear that something was amiss. Perhaps to cheer us up, my father said that he would finally make for my mother the set of furniture she had been asking him to make for a very long time now. In fact, the set of furniture had been a bone of contention between them. That brought a half-hearted, polite smile to my mother's face. Then, turning to me, my father asked what he could make for me.

It came into my mind without thinking. "A trunk," I said.

"But you have a trunk already. You have your mother's trunk," he said to me.

"Yes, but I want my own trunk," I said back.

"Very well. A trunk is your request, a trunk you will have," he said.

Out of the corner of one eye, I could see my mother. Out of the corner of the other eye, I could see her shadow on the wall, cast there by the lamp-light. It was a big and solid shadow, and it looked so much like my mother that I became frightened. For I could not be sure whether for the rest of my life I would be able to tell when it was really my mother and when it was really her shadow standing between me and the rest of the world.

Chapter Seven

The Long Rain

Days before it was decided that I was not well enough to go to school, I walked around feeling weak, as if at any moment I would collapse in a heap. If I rested my head on my desk, in an instant I fell asleep; the walk to and from school wore me out, so that I moved at the speed of an old jalopy. Nothing unusual seemed wrong. I did not have a fever. No wild storms raged through my stomach. My appetite was as poor as it had always been. My mother, tugging at my eyelids this way and that, could not see any signs of biliousness. All the same, I was in no condition to keep up in my usual way, so I had to take to my bed.

For over a year, no rain fell. There was nothing unusual about that; drought was such a big part of our life that no one would even make a comment on it. Then, each day for a week or so, the clouds overhead turned black. No rain came right away with the black clouds, but then one day it started to drizzle, first in that annoying way of a drizzle, where it stings your face and your hands and your feet. That went on for a few days, when suddenly the rain started to come down in a heavy torrent. The rain went on in this way for over three months. By the end of it, the sea had risen and what used to be dry land was covered with water, and crabs lived there. In spite of what everyone said, the sea never did go back to the way it had been, and what a great conversation piece it made to try and remember what used to be there where the sea now stretched up to.

In my small room. I lay on my pitch-pine bed, which, since I was sick, was made up with my Sunday sheets. I lay on my back and stared at the ceiling. I could hear the rain as it came down on the galvanized roof. The sound the rain made as it landed on the roof pressed me down in my bed, bolted me down, and I couldn't even so much as lift my head if my life depended on it. My mother and father, sometimes together, sometimes separately, stood at the foot of my bed and looked down at me. They spoke to each other. I couldn't hear what it was that they said, but I could see the words leave their mouths. The words traveled through the air toward me, but just as they reached my ears they would fall to the floor, suddenly dead. Most likely, my father said that it was all the studying I had been doing at school, that I had moved along from form to form too fast and it had taken a heavy toll. Most likely, my mother agreed, but she also would have said that, just to be sure, she would call Ma Jolie, an obeah woman from Dominica who now lived not far from our house, and who was recommended to my mother by her mother, Ma Chess, who still lived in Dominica. To the Ma Jolie idea, my father would have said, "Very well, but count me out; have her come when I am not here."

One afternoon, in the rain, my mother and father took me to the doctor, my father carrying me on his back, my mother walking by his side with her head bent down. The doctor, a man from England named Dr. Stephens, and my mother were one in their feeling against germs, parasites, and disease in general, with my mother always on the lookout for signs in my father and me of things to report to him. When I came down with a case of hookworm, Dr. Stephens and my mother had held discussions on the several ways in which I could have picked it up, finally settling on my bad habit of going about without my shoes on— against my mother's loudly expressed wishes. After he had pointed out to my mother the many places on a person's body where germs might lodge themselves, she made a habit of cutting my fingernails every Saturday. Dr. Stephens now examined me from head to foot, poking me here and there, listening to my heart, my lungs, taking my pulse and temperature, peering into my eyes and ears. In the end, he could find nothing much wrong, except that he thought I might be a little run-down. My mother asked herself out loud, "How could that be?" and then told Dr. Stephens that she certainly would redouble her efforts at making me eat properly, feeding me more beef tea, more barley water, more vitamins, more eggs and

milk, along with keeping me in bed until whatever it
was that had come over me went away.

Going home, there was the rain still. I could see the
huge drops as they hit the ground, but I couldn't hear
the sound they made. The streets were empty; everybody was inside, taking shelter. My head rested on my
father's shoulder, my arms were wrapped tightly
around his neck. I could feel that he drew extra breath
just from the burden of carrying me such a long distance. Sometimes he would turn his head to say something to my mother, but I couldn't make out what
that might be.

At home, my mother undressed me and put me to
bed. Soon after, she brought me an egg cordial with
two tablespoons of rum in it. Ordinarily, I had to be
coaxed to drink this, so much did I hate the taste of
rum mixed up with eggs, but I could not taste anything now, so it all went down with ease. My father
came in, looked at me, and said, "So, Little Miss, huh?
Hmmmm." I knew that he would say this before the
words came out of his mouth. When the words reached
me, the "So" was bigger than the "Little," and the
"Miss" was bigger than the "huh," and the "Hmmmm"
was bigger than all the other words rolled into one.
Then all the sound rocked back and forth in my ears,
and I had a picture of it; it looked like a large wave
constantly dashing up against a wall in the sea, and
the whole thing made me feel far away and weight-
less. I could hear the rain on the roof, and it was still
pinning me down. I looked inside my head. A black
thing was lying down there, and it shut out all my

memory of the things that had happened to me. I knew that in my fifteen years a lot of things had happened, but now I couldn't put my finger on a single thing. As I fell asleep, I had no feeling in any part of my body except the back of my skull, which felt as if it would split open and spew out huge red flames. I dreamed then that I was walking through warm air filled with soot, heading toward the sea. When I got there, I started to drink in the sea in huge great gulps, because I was so thirsty. I drank and drank until all that was left was the bare dry seabed. All the water from the sea filled me up, from my toes to my head, and I swelled up very big. But then little cracks began to appear in me and the water started to leak out—first in just little seeps and trickles coming out of my seams, then with a loud roar as I burst open. The water ran back and made up the sea again, and again I was walking through the warm soot—only this time wet and in tatters and not going anywhere in particular.

When I woke up, I was sitting in my father's lap and I was wearing a different nightie from the one I had fallen asleep in. My mother, dressed in her nightie, was bent over my bed, changing my sheets. I must have asked my father what was the matter, for he said to me, "You wet, Little Miss, you wet." My father was wearing only his undergarments, which by then I knew how to iron without leaving any un-wanted wrinkles. His clothes smelled of his perspiration from the day before. Through the folds of my nightie, I could feel the hair on his legs, and as I moved my own legs back and forth against his the hair on his legs made a swoosh, swoosh sound, like a brush being rubbed against wood. A funny feeling went through me that I liked and was frightened of at the same time, and I shuddered. At this, my father, thinking I was cold, hugged me even closer. It dawned on me then that my father, except for when he was sick, slept in no clothes at all, for he would never sleep in clothes he had worn the day before. I do not know why that lodged in my mind, but it did.

My mother finished making my bed, and she bent over and picked me up out of my father's lap. I was fifteen years old, but the two of them handled me as if I were just born. In bed, I looked at them standing over me. I couldn't hear the rain, but I knew it was still falling. My parents said things to each other, but I couldn't make out what they said, either.

When I opened my eyes in the morning (I knew it was morning, for a large white candle was lit, not my lamp), I saw my mother seated at the foot of my bed. Her head was tilted to one side, and she had a worried expression on her face. When she saw that I was looking at her, she smiled at me. She said, "How are you feeling today, Little Miss?" and "Did you sleep well?" Though I can't be sure, I must have answered in a way that pleased her, for she kept bobbing her head up and down and said, "Good." She had ready for me some soap and water in my basin, which stood on my washstand, and she helped me to brush my teeth and wash my face. She tried to comb my hair, but I must have cried out, because she then smoothed down my plaits and kissed my head. Propping me up in bed with some pillows, she placed on my lap a tray that had on it three pieces of bread; on the bread was a cheese spread made of grated cheddar cheese, eggs, and butter. Also on the tray was a cup of chocolate made with milk from which the cream had not been removed. This meal of bread and cheese spread, with chocolate in my milk (the chocolate came from my grandmother, Ma Chess, who grew the beans and then did all the steps herself to turn them into chocolate; she sent the chocolate to us in a big box, along with nutmeg and other spices, coffee, and almonds), was among the three or four things in the world that I most liked to eat. But now, looking at it, I only knew that I had liked eating it at some point in my life and that it was usually given to me for supper on Tuesdays, when I came home from Brownie meetings.

Outside me, the word "Brownie" hung just before my eyes. Inside me, the black thing that was lodged in my head grew even more leaden. A part of the black thing broke away, as if it had been dropped to the ground, and a small yellow light took its place. Inside the yellow light, I was a Brownie, a small toy Brownie. It was me, all right, but made small. In truth, I belonged to the First Division troop of Brownies, which meant that in parades my troop marched ahead of all the other Brownie troops. A woman named Miss Herbert was our leader. She was a cashier in the hardware-and-lumber department of a store called George W. Bennet Bryson & Sons, and whenever I

accompanied my father to that store, where he sometimes bought supplies, she would wait on us. I would
curtsy to her in the special way that I was supposed to
curtsy to anyone whom my parents had made a kind
of guardian for me in their absence, and she would
acknowledge me, though in a sort of gruff way, to
show that even though I was a good Brownie, who won
many citations for good deeds, I was not particularly
in with her. She always said that she respected and
liked us all equally, and I have to say that that attitude
didn't go down well with me, accustomed as I was to
being singled out and held up in a special way. Our
troop was divided into four groups of seven girls each:
elves, pixies, fairies, and gnomes. I was an elf, so I
wore an emblem of a mischievous, dancing elf just
above the left breast pocket of my uniform. On my
sleeves and on my shoulders I wore all sorts of stripes
and other emblems and badges to show that I had
excelled in one thing or another. On our yellow ties
we wore a brass badge in the shape of a four-leaf
clover. We began our meetings with the whole troop
standing in the yard of the Methodist church, forming a circle around the flagpole, our eyes following
the Union Jack as it was raised up; then we swore
allegiance to our country, by which was meant England. For an hour and a half, we did all sorts of
Brownie things; then we gathered again around the
flagpole to lower the flag and swear allegiance. Just
before we parted, we crouched down with our hands
on our shoulders, two fingers pointing up, and we
said in unison, "Tu-whoo, tu-whit, tu-whoo," in imi-

tation of the wise old owl that was the patron of our troop, and it was wished for us that as we grew old we would grow wise also.

Lying on my sickbed, I saw the toy Brownie who was also me on the road going to and from Brownie meetings. I was all alone. There were no other Brownies around me; there were no other people around me; there was only me, coming and going on the big road, which remained its normal size. I didn't know how long it would take me to come and go with my little toy steps. As I watched myself long and hard, I forgot everything, but eventually I could hear my mother's voice. I still couldn't make out what she was saying, but I could see some of the words as they landed in the air between us. There was "imagine," "that," "most," "nicely," "because," "down," "little," "basket," "connive," "well," "trust," "behavior," "beads," "beasts," "blight." They danced around, in and out, as if around a maypole. Settling back in my bed, I looked up at the beams in the ceiling. I then sat on one of them and looked down at my mother and me. I closed my eyes, and the warm, black soot started to fall. I fell asleep.

The rain continued to come, sometimes in a heavy drizzle, sometimes as if, all along, we had been living with a dam overhead and someone had purposely made a huge gash in it. My father could no longer go off to work, so he built furniture in his shop. One day, he arranged to be somewhere else and Ma Jolie came. She made cross marks on the soles of my feet, on my knees, on my stomach, in my armpits, and on my forehead. She lit two special candles and placed one over the head of my bed and the other near the foot. She said that, with all the rain, it was impossible for anything meaning me harm to be living outside in the yard, so she would not even bother to look there now. She burned some incense in one corner of my room. She put a dozen tiny red candles —with white paper on their bottoms, to keep them afloat—in a basin of thick yellow oil. When she lit them, they threw a beautiful pink glow all over my room. In the basin with the candles she had placed scraps of paper on which were written the names of people who had wanted to harm me, most of them women my father had loved a long time ago. She told my mother, after a careful look around, that there were no spirits in my room or in any other part of the house, and that all the things she did were just a precaution in case anyone should get ideas on hearing that I was in such a weakened condition. Before she left, she pinned a little black sachet, filled with something that smelled abominable, to the inside of my nightie, and she gave my mother some little vials filled with fluids to rub on me at different times of the day. My mother placed them on my shelf, right alongside the bottles of compounds of vitamins and purgatives that Dr. Stephens had prescribed. When my father came in to see me. he looked at all my medicines—Dr. Stephens's and Ma Jolie's—lined up side by side and screwed up his face, the way he did when he didn't like what he saw. He must have said something to my mother, for she arranged the shelf in a new way, with Dr. Stephens's prescriptions in the front and Ma Jolie's prescriptions in the back.

For the first two weeks of my condition, my mother and father did not live a regular life. They were up with me at all hours of the night, and my mother was afraid to leave me alone in the day. But then they must have suddenly decided to take everything in stride, and, without making too much of it, they went back to their usual routines. The rain was still falling, but my father went back to work, leaving our house at the stroke of seven by the Anglican church bell. One day, my mother left me alone and went to the fish market for the fish that was to be our dinner that night. Just before she left, she said, "Little Miss, try and get some rest"—the main thing both my parents said to me now.

Once I was alone, suddenly some photographs that were in frames and arranged in a semicircle on the little table not far from my bed loomed up big in front of me. There was a picture of me in my white dress school uniform. There was a picture of me as a bridesmaid at my Aunt Mary's marriage to Monsieur Pacquet. There was a picture of my father wearing his white cricket uniform, holding a bat with one hand, the other arm wrapped tightly around my mother's waist. There was a picture of me in the white dress in which I had just been received into church and took Communion for the first time, wearing shoes that had a decorative cutout on the sides. When I had bought those shoes and showed them to my mother, she said that they were not fit for a young lady and not fit for wearing on being received into church. We had an enormous fight over the shoes, and I may have said unspeakable things to her, though I have forgotten everything except that at the end I turned and said, "I wish you were dead." As I said it, I felt hollow inside. My mother then got such a bad headache that the turtleberry leaves she placed on her temples to draw out the pain had to be changed every two hours, so quickly did the heat of the pain scorch them. That night, I could hear her making some moaning sounds as she paced up and down the house, because the pain kept her awake. When she stopped, I was sure that she had died, and that the new sounds I heard were the sounds of the undertaker, Mr. Straffee, come to remove her body for burial.

The photographs, as they stood on the table, now began to blow themselves up until they touched the ceiling and then shrink back down, but to a size that I could not easily see. They did this with a special regularity, keeping beat to a music I was not privy to. Up and down they went, up and down. They did this for so long that they began to perspire quite a bit, and when they finally stopped, falling back on the table limp with exhaustion, the smell coming from them was unbearable to me. I got out of bed, gathered them up in my arms, took them over to the basin of water on the washstand, and gave them a good bath. I washed them thoroughly with soap and water, digging into all the crevices, trying, with not much success, to straighten out the creases in Aunt Mary's veil, trying, with not much success, to remove the dirt from the front of my father's trousers. When I finished, I dried them thoroughly, dusted them with talcum powder, and then laid them down in a corner covered with a blanket, so that they would be warm while they slept. I got back into bed, and I must have fallen asleep, for the sound of my mother's voice—a worried bleat, really—brought me back to just lying in my bed and looking up at the ceiling.

My mother was on her hands and knees, trying to dry up the floor. When I washed the pictures, I had spilled water all over, and my nightie and my sheets were wet. The pictures were in a little heap off to one side of the room, and even in my state I could see that they were completely ruined. None of the people in the wedding picture, except for me, had any face left. In the picture of my mother and father, I had erased them from the waist down. In the picture of me wearing my confirmation dress, I had erased all of myself except for the shoes. When my father came home, I heard him say, "Poor Miss, she can't even be left alone for a short while."

So, once again, my mother arranged her duties in such a way that I was never left alone. A neighbor did her grocery shopping for her. Another neighbor was sent to market to buy our daily fresh provisions. The fish we ate regularly for our dinner was brought to us, already scaled, by either Mr. Earl or Mr. Nigel, the two fishermen who supplied us.

One day, Mr. Nigel brought the fish, and after a little chat with my mother he came in to see me and to wish me a quick recovery. Since he was still wearing his fishing clothes (khaki trousers that were beautifully mended with patches all over, an old red chambray shirt) and covered with fish scales and blood, he remained in the doorway of my room and said a few things. I couldn't make out all that he said, but I could see that he had brought me a fish that somehow he believed was my favorite. How pleased he looked and how happy. Of the two fishermen, I had always liked him better. He reminded me of my father. He was quiet and thoughtful in the same way, and he liked being a fisherman the way my father liked being a carpenter. As I was thinking of how much he reminded me of my father, the words "You are just like Mr. John" came out of my mouth.

He laughed and said, "Now, mind, I don't tell him you say that." His laugh then filled up the whole room, and it sucked up all the air, so that I had no air to breathe, only Mr. Nigel's laugh, and it filled up my nostrils, my throat, my lungs, and it went all the way down until every empty space in me was just filled up with Mr. Nigel's laugh. In this state, when I looked at him I could see all sorts of things.

My father's great-grandfather had been a fisherman, but he must have been a bad fisherman, for he never caught many fish in his fishpots. One day when he went out to search his pots, he found the usual two or three small fish, and it made him so angry that he picked up the fish, said to God to kiss his backside, and threw the fish back in the water. A curse fell on him, and shortly thereafter he took very ill and died. Just before he died, his skin burst open, as if he were an overfull pea shell, and his last words were "Dem damn fish." I could see Mr. Nigel and Mr. Earl sitting under a tree, their heads bent over a net that they were mending, one starting a sentence, the other finishing it. Mr. Nigel and Mr. Earl shared everything. At sea, they shared the same boat, the same catch. At home, they shared the same house, with Mr. Earl's entrance from the street and Mr. Nigel's entrance through the yard. The house had a door inside that connected their two parts, but the door was never locked. They shared the same wife, a woman named Miss Catherine, and though she did not live with them completely, her own house was just a few doors away, and she visited them quite regularly, sometimes entering from the street, sometimes entering through the yard. There, Miss Catherine cooked food, and the three of them, sitting at a table, ate from the same pot with their bare hands. That was a sight all could see as they passed by. I liked Miss Catherine, because she used snuff, and it made her spit, and her way of spitting seemed as if it was the best way such a thing could be done. My mother did not like Miss Catherine, because she was barren, slightly crippled, and was always telling my mother the proper way to bring me up. My mother, though she thought this a secret, also did not like her sister, my Aunt Mary, and whenever they had a quarrel, usually by letter, my mother would call her a barren, crippled, interfering idiot. My aunt was barren, was crippled, and constantly told my mother how to bring me up. I never knew if Miss Catherine was a cripple from the day she was born, or if as a child she had had an accident, or if someone had willed her that way.

When Mr. Nigel laughed and his laughing turned out to have such an effect on me, I leaped out of bed and cast myself at him with such force that it threw him to the ground. Then, in a burst of chat, I told him all these things as they rushed through my mind: about my father's great-grandfather, and about himself and Mr. Earl and Miss Catherine. He took it all in as if he were a disinterested party, as if it were all news to him.

I don't know how long it was after this that Ma Chess appeared. I heard my mother and father wonder to each other how she came to us, for she appeared on a day when the steamer was not due, and so they didn't go to meet her at the jetty. She and my mother stood at the foot of my bed looking down at me and whispering to each other. They tugged at and smoothed down each other's clothes when they wanted to make a particular point. When Ma Chess leaned over me, she smelled of many different things, all of them even more abominable than the black sachet Ma Jolie had pinned to my nightie. Whatever Ma Jolie knew, my grandmother knew at least ten times more. How she regretted that my mother didn't show more of an interest in obeah things. Ma Chess never took a bath in just plain water and soap. She took a bath,

once a month or so, in water in which things animal
and vegetable had been boiled for a long time. Before
she took this bath, she first swam in the sea. As she
leaned over me now, she poked in the same way Ma
Jolie had. Then she said to my mother, in French
patois, "Not like Johnnie. Not like Johnnie at all."
She stood at my mother's side again, and they continued to tug at and smooth down each other's clothes.

When my mother was thirteen years old, her
brother John died. He was twenty-three then. My
mother and her sister worshipped him, his own
mother worshipped him, and after he died they all
said that life would never be the same. They talked
so much about him and in such a way that sometimes
I was sure that he had just stepped out on an errand
and would be returning at any moment now, that I
would see him rounding the corner with the special
gait they said he had of skipping along every few steps.
Almost everything he ever owned or wore was kept
in a large trunk in Ma Chess's room, and when I went
to visit her, Ma Chess, pretending to air out the things
in the trunk, would show all of it as if it were part of
a great exhibition. When they spoke of him to me,
they would say "your Uncle Johnnie," as if he hadn't
died long before I was born. My mother remembered
all the jokes and games he played with her so well
that she played the same jokes and games with me, and
if I seemed not to understand what was happening
she would say, "Well, your Uncle Johnnie did that to
me," to clear up the mystery. My Aunt Mary married
a man, Monsieur Pacquet, her parents could not stand,

but he was a man Uncle Johnnie had met in Roseau
when taking in a crop of green figs and had spoken
extremely well of to his sister. When Uncle Johnnie
got sick, Ma Chess was sure that a doctor was the last
thing he needed. Pa Chess was sure that a doctor was
the one thing he needed, and Pa Chess got his way.
For two years, Uncle Johnnie lay in bed, each day
looking rosier and rosier. Then one day he died. On
the day he died, he had never looked better. When he
died, a large worm bored its way out of his leg and
rested on his shinbone. Then it, too, died. From that
day on, Ma Chess never spoke to Pa Chess again, even
though they lived in the same house. She never said
a word for him or against him, and if his name came
up she would absent herself in spirit—and in body,
too, if his name continued to come up. Pa Chess not
only oversaw everything about the funeral, he even
preached a sermon—the usual thing: about everything happening for the best, people meeting again
and living in eternal bliss. Ma Chess did not attend
the funeral, though she visited the grave on special
occasions. She had all her clothes made up in black
cloth—the only color she wore from that day on.

Ma Chess settled in on the floor at the foot of my
bed, eating and sleeping there, and soon I grew to
count on her smells and the sound her breath made
as it went in and out of her body. Sometimes at night,
when I would feel that I was all locked up in the
warm falling soot and could not find my way out, Ma
Chess would come into my bed with me and stay until
I was myself—whatever that had come to be by then

—again. I would lie on my side, curled up like a little comma, and Ma Chess would lie next to me, curled up like a bigger comma, into which I fit. In the daytime, while my mother attended my father, keeping him company as he ate, Ma Chess fed me my food, coaxing me to take mouthful after mouthful. She bathed me and changed my clothes and sheets and did all the other things that my mother used to do. Ma Chess and my father kept out of each other's way —not so much because they didn't like each other but because they didn't see the world in the same way. Ma Chess once asked my father to tell her exactly what it was he really did, and when he said that he was off to build a house she said, "A house? Why live in a house? All you need is a nice hole in the ground, so you can come and go as you please."

It rained every day for three and a half months, and for all of those days I was sick in bed. I knew quite well that I did not have the power to make the atmosphere feel as sick as I felt, but still I couldn't help putting the two together. For one day, just as mysteriously as my sickness came, so it left. At the same time, just as mysteriously as the rain came, so it left. It stopped raining for a day, it stopped raining for two days, and then it stopped raining altogether. Drought returned, and, except that the sea was bigger than it used to be, everything was the same again. When the sun started to come out once more, my windows were thrown open and the heat and light rushed in. I had to shield my eyes, I was so unused to seeing everything. The rain had ruined my mother's garden and some fruit trees; a few clothes my mother forgot in her ironing basket had grown mildew; and a foundation for a house my father was building had washed away. My mother restored her garden and the fruit trees; she knew of a way to remove mildew from clothes, and they were restored also. My father put in a new foundation and continued building the house. When it became quite clear that I really was getting better, Ma Chess left, and in the way she came, too: with no announcement and on a day when the steamer was not due in port.

One day, I was taken outside for the first time in a long while. When I stepped on the ground, it didn't move. The sounds I heard didn't pass through me, forming a giant, angry funnel. The things I saw stayed in their places. My mother sat me down under a tree, and I watched a boy she had paid sixpence climb up a coconut tree to get me some coconuts. My mother looked at my pinched, washed-out face and said, "Poor Little Miss, you look so sad." Just at that moment, I was not feeling sad at all. I was feeling how much I never wanted to see a boy climb a coconut tree again, how much I never wanted to see the sun shine day in, day out again, how much I never wanted to see my mother bent over a pot cooking me something that she felt would do me good when I ate it, how much I never wanted to feel her long, bony fingers against my cheek again, how much I never wanted to hear her voice in my ear again, how much I longed to be in a place where nobody knew a thing about me and liked me for just that reason, how much the whole world into which I was born had become an unbearable burden and I wished I could reduce it to some small thing that I could hold underwater until it died. Disguising how I felt, I looked up at my mother, tilted my head to one side, and smiled, and this pleased her. Walking back to my room, my mother and I both silently noticed that I now towered over her. I was so unused to this that I made my already stooped back—which came from bad posture, and which no amount of scolding could cure—look even more so. During my sickness, I had grown to a considerable height—almost equal to my grandmother's. In bed now, I had to double myself up to fit properly.

Soon I was able to return to school. Because of my new height, I needed new uniforms and new shoes, for my feet had grown also. I had the skirt of my uniform made to a length that ended just below my calves. No one quarreled with this, for we were always being urged not to show our legs. I could not do anything about my shoes, for we could wear only one special kind bought at one special store, but I bought a hat whose crown and brim were too big for me, and when I wore it my head was held down and it was hard to see my face. Walking to and from school, my long-skirt uniform hanging on my thin form, my head held down, my back curved in an exaggerated stoop, one arm held behind me and resting on my lower back, the other anchoring the bag that held my books, each step I took purposely timid, I created such a picture that apparently everyone talked about me. Or so

I was told by Gwen, formerly the love of my life, now reduced to an annoying acquaintance. Along with all that, I acquired a strange accent—at least, no one had ever heard anyone talk that way before—and some other tricks. If someone behaved toward me in a way that didn't meet with my approval, without saying a word I would look at them directly with one eyebrow raised. I always got an apology. If someone asked me a question, I would begin my answer with the words "Actually" or "As a matter of fact." It had the effect of allowing no room for doubt. I left people's company if they said or did something I did not care for, and I had made my presence so felt that when I removed myself my absence was felt, too. Many girls wanted to show me up, and tried, but all attempts failed. I could see that everything about me aroused envy and discontent, and that made me happy—the only happiness I knew then. I never mentioned my sickness, and if the subject came up I made the appearance of not caring to talk about it. When I finally wished to say something, I would say, "During the time of my illness." How I loved the sound of the words as they rolled off my tongue, and it wasn't long before I made all the other girls wish that they would get sick also.

Chapter Eight

A Walk to the Jetty

"My name is Annie John." These were the first words that came into my mind as I woke up on the morning of the last day I spent in Antigua, and they stayed there, lined up one behind the other, marching up and down, for I don't know how long. At noon on that day, a ship on which I was to be a passenger would sail to Barbados, and there I would board another ship, which would sail to England, where I would study to become a nurse. My name was the last thing I saw the night before, just as I was falling asleep; it was written in big, black letters all over my trunk, sometimes followed by my address in Antigua, sometimes followed by my address as it would be in England. I did not want to go to England, I did not want to be a nurse, but I would have chosen going off to live in a cavern and keeping house for seven unruly men rather than go on with my life as it stood. I never wanted to lie in this bed again, my legs hanging out way past the foot of it, tossing and turning on my mattress, with its cotton stuffing all lumped just where it wasn't a good place to be lumped. I never wanted to lie in my bed again and hear Mr. Ephraim driving his sheep to pasture—a signal to my mother that she should get up to prepare my father's and my bath and breakfast. I never wanted to lie in my bed and hear her get dressed, washing her face, brushing her teeth, and gargling. I especially never wanted to lie in my bed and hear my mother gargling again.

Lying there in the half-dark of my room, I could see my shelf, with my books—some of them prizes I had won in school, some of them gifts from my mother —and with photographs of people I was supposed to love forever no matter what, and with my old thermos, which was given to me for my eighth birthday, and some shells I had gathered at different times I spent at the sea. In one corner stood my washstand and its beautiful basin of white enamel with blooming red hibiscus painted at the bottom and an urn that matched. In another corner were my old school shoes and my Sunday shoes. In still another corner, a bureau held my old clothes. I knew everything in this room, inside out and outside in. I had lived in this room for thirteen of my seventeen years. I could see in my mind's eye even the day my father was adding it onto the rest of the house. Everywhere I looked stood something that had meant a lot to me, that had given me pleasure at some point, or could remind me of a time that was a happy time. But as I was lying there my heart could have burst open with joy at the thought of never having to see any of it again.

If someone had asked me for a little summing up of my life at that moment as I lay in bed, I would have said, "My name is Annie John. I was born on the fifteenth of September, seventeen years ago, at Holberton Hospital, at five o'clock in the morning. At the time I was born, the moon was going down at one end of the sky and the sun was coming up at the other. My mother's name is Annie also. My father's name is Alexander, and he is thirty-five years older than my mother. Two of his children are four and six years older than she is. Looking at how sickly he has become and looking at the way my mother now has to run up and down for him, gathering the herbs and barks that he boils in water, which he drinks instead of the medicine the doctor has ordered for him, I plan not only never to marry an old man but certainly never to marry at all. The house we live in my father built with his own hands. The bed I am lying in my father built with his own hands. If I get up and sit on a chair, it is a chair my father built with his own hands. When my mother uses a large wooden spoon to stir the porridge we sometimes eat as part of our breakfast, it will be a spoon that my father has carved with his own hands. The sheets on my bed my mother made with her own hands. The curtains hanging at my window my mother made with her own hands. The nightie I am wearing, with scalloped neck and hem and sleeves, my mother made with her own hands. When I look at things in a certain way, I suppose I should say that the two of them made me with their own hands. For most of my life, when the three of us went anywhere together I stood between the two of them or sat between the two of them. But then I got too big, and there I was, shoulder to shoulder with them more or less, and it became not very comfortable to walk down the street together. And so now there they are together and here I am apart. I don't see them now the way I used to, and I don't love them now the way I used to. The bitter thing about it is that they are just the same and it is I who have changed, so all the things I used to be and all the things I used to feel are as false as the teeth in my father's head. Why, I wonder, didn't I see the hypocrite in my mother when, over the years, she said that she loved me and could hardly live without me, while at the same time proposing and arranging separation after separation, including this one, which, unbeknownst to her, *I* have arranged to be permanent? So now I, too, have hypocrisy, and breasts (small ones), and hair growing in the appropriate places, and sharp eyes, and I have made a vow never to be fooled again."

Lying in my bed for the last time, I thought, This is what I add up to. At that, I felt as if someone had placed me in a hole and was forcing me first down and then up against the pressure of gravity. I shook myself and prepared to get up. I said to myself, "I am getting up out of this bed for the last time." Everything I would do that morning until I got on the ship that would take me to England I would be doing for the last time, for I had made up my mind that, come what may, the road for me now went only in one direction: away from my home, away from my mother, away from my father, away from the everlasting blue sky, away from the everlasting hot sun, away from people who said to me, "This happened during the time your mother was carrying you." If I had been asked to put into words why I felt this way, if I had been given years to reflect and come up with the words of why I felt this way, I would not have been able to come up with so much as the letter "A." I only knew that I felt the way I did, and that this feeling was the strongest thing in my life.

The Anglican church bell struck seven. My father had already bathed and dressed and was in his workshop puttering around. As if the day of my leaving were something to celebrate, they were treating it as a holiday, and nothing in the usual way would take place. My father would not go to work at all. When I got up, my mother greeted me with a big, bright "Good morning"—so big and bright that I shrank before it. I bathed quickly in some warm bark water that my mother had prepared for me. I put on my underclothes—all of them white and all of them smelling funny. Along with my earrings, my neck chain, and my bracelets, all made of gold from British Guiana, my underclothes had been sent to my mother's obeah woman, and whatever she had done to my jewelry and underclothes would help protect me from evil spirits and every kind of misfortune. The things I never wanted to see or hear or do again now made up at least three weeks' worth of grocery lists. I placed a mark against obeah women, jewelry, and white under-clothes. Over my underclothes, I put on an around-the-yard dress of my mother's. The clothes I would wear for my voyage were a dark-blue pleated skirt and a blue-and-white checked blouse (the blue in the blouse matched exactly the blue of my skirt) with a large sailor collar and with a tie made from the same material as the skirt—a blouse that came down a long way past my waist, over my skirt. They were lying on a chair, freshly ironed by my mother. Putting on my clothes was the last thing I would do just before leav-ing the house. Miss Cornelia came and pressed my hair and then shaped it into what felt like a hundred corkscrews, all lying flat against my head so that my hat would fit properly.

At breakfast, I was seated in my usual spot, with my mother at one end of the table, my father at the other, and me in the middle, so that as they talked to me or to each other I would shift my head to the left or to the right and get a good look at them. We were having a Sunday breakfast, a breakfast as if we had just come back from Sunday-morning services: salt fish and antroba and souse and hard-boiled eggs, and even special Sunday bread from Mr. Daniel, our baker. On Sundays, we ate this big breakfast at eleven o'clock and then we didn't eat again until four o'clock, when we had our big Sunday dinner. It was the best break-fast we ate, and the only breakfast better than that was the one we ate on Christmas morning. My parents were in a festive mood, saying what a wonderful time

I would have in my new life, what a wonderful opportunity this was for me, and what a lucky person I was. They were eating away as they talked, my father's false teeth making that clop-clop sound like a horse on a walk as he talked, my mother's mouth going up and down like a donkey's as she chewed each mouthful thirty-two times. (I had long ago counted, because it was something she made me do also, and I was trying to see if this was just one of her rules that applied only to me.) I was looking at them with a smile on my face but disgust in my heart when my mother said, "Of course, you are a young lady now, and we won't be surprised if in due time you write to say that one day soon you are to be married."

Without thinking, I said, with bad feeling that I didn't hide very well, "How absurd!"

My parents immediately stopped eating and looked at me as if they had not seen me before. My father was the first to go back to his food. My mother continued to look. I don't know what went through her mind, but I could see her using her tongue to dislodge food stuck in the far corners of her mouth.

Many of my mother's friends now came to say goodbye to me, and to wish me God's blessings. I thanked them and showed the proper amount of joy at the glorious things they pointed out to me that my future held and showed the proper amount of sorrow at how much my parents and everyone else who loved me would miss me. My body ached a little at all this false going back and forth, at all this taking in of people gazing at me with heads tilted, love and pity on their smiling faces. I could have left without saying any goodbyes to them and I wouldn't have missed it. There was only one person I felt I should say goodbye to, and that was my former friend Gwen. We had long ago drifted apart, and when I saw her now my heart nearly split in two with embarrassment at the feelings I used to have for her and things I had shared with her. She had now degenerated into complete silliness, hardly able to complete a sentence without putting in a few giggles. Along with the giggles, she had developed some other schoolgirl traits that she did not have when she was actually a schoolgirl, so beneath her were such things then. When we were saying our goodbyes, it was all I could do not to say cruelly, "Why are you behaving like such a monkey?" Instead, I put everything on a friendly plain, wishing her well and the best in the future. It was then that she told me that she was more or less engaged to a boy she had known while growing up early on in Nevis, and that soon, in a year or so, they would be married. My reply to her was "Good luck," and she thought I meant her well, so she grabbed me and said, "Thank you. I knew you would be happy about it." But to me it was as if she had shown me a high point from which she was going to jump and hoped to land in one piece on her feet. We parted, and when I turned away I didn't look back.

My mother had arranged with a stevedore to take my trunk to the jetty ahead of me. At ten o'clock on the dot, I was dressed, and we set off for the jetty.

An hour after that, I would board a launch that would take me out to sea, where I then would board the ship. Starting out, as if for old time's sake and without giving it a thought, we lined up in the old way: I walking between my mother and my father. I loomed way above my father and could see the top of his head. We must have made a strange sight: a grown girl all dressed up in the middle of a morning, in the middle of the week, walking in step in the middle between her two parents, for people we didn't know stared at us. It was all of half an hour's walk from our house to the jetty, but I was passing through most of the years of my life. We passed by the house where Miss Dulcie, the seamstress that I had been apprenticed to for a time, lived, and just as I was passing by, a wave of bad feeling for her came over me, because I suddenly remembered that the months I spent with her all she had me do was sweep the floor, which was always full of threads and pins and needles, and I never seemed to sweep it clean enough to please her. Then she would send me to the store to buy buttons or thread, though I was only allowed to do this if I was given a sample of the button or thread, and then she would find fault even though they were an exact match of the samples she had given me. And all the while she said to me, "A girl like you will never learn to sew properly, you know." At the time, I don't suppose I minded it, because it was customary to treat the first-year apprentice with such scorn, but now I placed on the dustheap of my life Miss Dulcie and everything that I had had to do with her.

We were soon on the road that I had taken to
school, to church, to Sunday school, to choir practice,
to Brownie meetings, to Girl Guide meetings, to meet
a friend. I was five years old when I first walked on
this road unaccompanied by someone to hold my
hand. My mother had placed three pennies in my
little basket, which was a duplicate of her bigger
basket, and sent me to the chemist's shop to buy a
pennyworth of senna leaves, a pennyworth of eucalyptus leaves, and a pennyworth of camphor. She then instructed me on what side of the road to walk, where
to make a turn, where to cross, how to look carefully
before I crossed, and if I met anyone that I knew to
politely pass greetings and keep on my way. I was
wearing a freshly ironed yellow dress that had printed
on it scenes of acrobats flying through the air and
swinging on a trapeze. I had just had a bath, and after
it, instead of powdering me with my baby-smelling
talcum powder, my mother had, as a special favor, let
me use her own talcum powder, which smelled quite
perfumy and came in a can that had painted on it
people going out to dinner in nineteenth-century
London and was called Mazie. How it pleased me to
walk out the door and bend my head down to sniff at
myself and see that I smelled just like my mother. I
went to the chemist's shop, and he had to come from
behind the counter and bend down to hear what it
was that I wanted to buy, my voice was so little and
timid then. I went back just the way I had come, and
when I walked into the yard and presented my basket
with its three packages to my mother, her eyes filled

with tears and she swooped me up and held me high in the air and said that I was wonderful and good and that there would never be anybody better. If I had just conquered Persia, she couldn't have been more proud of me.

We passed by our church—the church in which I had been christened and received and had sung in the junior choir. We passed by a house in which a girl I used to like and was sure I couldn't live without had lived. Once, when she had mumps, I went to visit her against my mother's wishes, and we sat on her bed and ate the cure of roasted, buttered sweet potatoes that had been placed on her swollen jaws, held there by a piece of white cloth. I don't know how, but my mother found out about it, and I don't know how, but she put an end to our friendship. Shortly after, the girl moved with her family across the sea to somewhere else. We passed the doll store, where I would go with my mother when I was little and point out the doll I wanted that year for Christmas. We passed the store where I bought the much-fought-over shoes I wore to church to be received in. We passed the bank. On my sixth birthday, I was given, among other things, the present of a sixpence. My mother and I then went to this bank, and with the sixpence I opened my own savings account. I was given a little gray book with my name in big letters on it, and in the balance column it said "6d." Every Saturday morning after that, I was given a sixpence—later a shilling, and later a two-and-sixpence piece—and I would take it to the bank for deposit. I had never been allowed to withdraw even a farthing from my bank account until just a few weeks before I was to leave; then the whole account was closed out, and I received from the bank the sum of six pounds ten shillings and two and a half pence.

We passed the office of the doctor who told my mother three times that I did not need glasses, that if my eyes were feeling weak a glass of carrot juice a day would make them strong again. This happened when I was eight. And so every day at recess I would run to my school gate and meet my mother, who was waiting for me with a glass of juice from carrots she had just grated and then squeezed, and I would drink it and then run back to meet my chums. I knew there was nothing at all wrong with my eyes, but I had recently read a story in *The Schoolgirl's Own Annual* in which the heroine, a girl a few years older than I was then, cut such a figure to my mind with the way she was always adjusting her small, round, horn-rimmed glasses that I felt I must have a pair exactly like them. When it became clear that I didn't need glasses, I began to complain about the glare of the sun being too much for my eyes, and I walked around with my hands shielding them—especially in my mother's presence. My mother then bought for me a pair of sunglasses with the exact horn-rimmed frames I wanted, and how I enjoyed the gestures of blowing on the lenses, wiping them with the hem of my uniform, adjusting the glasses when they slipped down my nose, and just removing them from their case and putting them on. In three weeks, I grew tired of them and they found a nice resting place in a drawer, along with some other things that at one time or another I couldn't live without.

We passed the store that sold only grooming aids, all imported from England. This store had in it a large porcelain dog—white, with black spots all over and a red ribbon of satin tied around its neck. The dog sat in front of a white porcelain bowl that was always filled with fresh water, and it sat in such a way that it looked as if it had just taken a long drink. When I was a small child, I would ask my mother, if ever we were near this store, to please take me to see the dog, and I would stand in front of it, bent over slightly, my hands resting on my knees, and stare at it and stare at it. I thought this dog more beautiful and more real than any actual dog I had ever seen or any actual dog I would ever see. I must have outgrown my interest in the dog, for when it disappeared I never asked what became of it. We passed the library, and if there was anything on this walk that I might have wept over leaving, this most surely would have been the thing. My mother had been a member of the library long before I was born. And since she took me everywhere with her when I was quite little, when she went to the library she took me along there, too. I would sit in her lap very quietly as she read books that she did not want to take home with her. I could not read the words yet, but just the way they looked on the page was interesting to me. Once, a book she was reading had a large picture of a man in it, and when I asked her who he was she told me that he was Louis Pasteur and that the book was about his life. It stuck in my mind, because she said it was because of him that she boiled my milk to purify it before I was allowed to drink it, that it was his idea, and that that was why the process was called pasteurization. One of the things I had put away in my mother's old trunk in which she kept all my childhood things was my library card. At that moment, I owed sevenpence in overdue fees.

As I passed by all these places, it was as if I were in a dream, for I didn't notice the people coming and going in and out of them, I didn't feel my feet touch ground, I didn't even feel my own body—I just saw these places as if they were hanging in the air, not having top or bottom, and as if I had gone in and out of them all in the same moment. The sun was bright; the sky was blue and just above my head. We then arrived at the jetty.

My heart now beat fast, and no matter how hard I tried, I couldn't keep my mouth from falling open and my nostrils from spreading to the ends of my face. My old fear of slipping between the boards of the jetty and falling into the dark-green water where the dark-green eels lived came over me. When my father's stomach started to go bad, the doctor had recommended a walk every evening right after he ate his dinner. Sometimes he would take me with him. When he took me with him, we usually went to the jetty, and there he would sit and talk to the night watchman about cricket or some other thing that aidn't interest me, because it was not personal; they didn't talk about their wives, or their children, or their parents, or about any of their likes and dislikes. They talked about things in such a strange way, and I didn't see what they found funny, but sometimes they made each other laugh so much that their guffaws would bound out to sea and send back an echo. I was always sorry when we got to the jetty and saw that the night watchman on duty was the one he enjoyed speaking to; it was like being locked up in a book filled with numbers and diagrams and what-ifs. For the thing about not being able to understand and enjoy what they were saying was I had nothing to take my mind off my fear of slipping in between the boards of the jetty.

Now, too, I had nothing to take my mind off what was happening to me. My mother and my father—I was leaving them forever. My home on an island—I was leaving it forever. What to make of everything? I felt a familiar hollow space inside. I felt I was being held down against my will. I felt I was burning up from head to toe. I felt that someone was tearing me up into little pieces and soon I would be able to see all the little pieces as they floated out into nothing in the deep blue sea. I didn't know whether to laugh or cry. I could see that it would be better not to think too clearly about any one thing. The launch was being made ready to take me, along with some other passengers, out to the ship that was anchored in the sea. My father paid our fares, and we joined a line of people waiting to board. My mother checked my bag to make sure that I had my passport, the

money she had given me, and a sheet of paper placed
between some pages in my Bible on which were
written the names of the relatives—people I had not
known existed—with whom I would live in England.
Across from the jetty was a wharf, and some steve-
dores were loading and unloading barges. I don't
know why seeing that struck me so, but suddenly a
wave of strong feeling came over me, and my heart
swelled with a great gladness as the words "I shall
never see this again" spilled out inside me. But then,
just as quickly, my heart shriveled up and the words
"I shall never see this again" stabbed at me. I don't
know what stopped me from falling in a heap at my
parents' feet.

When we were all on board, the launch headed out
to sea. Away from the jetty, the water became the
customary blue, and the launch left a wide path in
it that looked like a road. I passed by sounds and
smells that were so familiar that I had long ago
stopped paying any attention to them. But now here
they were, and the ever-present "I shall never see this
again" bobbed up and down inside me. There was
the sound of the seagull diving down into the water
and coming up with something silverish in its mouth.
There was the smell of the sea and the sight of small
pieces of rubbish floating around in it. There were
boats filled with fishermen coming in early. There
was the sound of their voices as they shouted greetings to each other. There was the hot sun, there was
the blue sea, there was the blue sky. Not very far
away, there was the white sand of the shore, with the

run-down houses all crowded in next to each other, for in some places only poor people lived near the shore. I was seated in the launch between my parents, and when I realized that I was gripping their hands tightly I glanced quickly to see if they were looking at me with scorn, for I felt sure that they must have known of my never-see-this-again feelings. But instead my father kissed me on the forehead and my mother kissed me on the mouth, and they both gave over their hands to me, so that I could grip them as much as I wanted. I was on the verge of feeling that it had all been a mistake, but I remembered that I wasn't a child anymore, and that now when I made up my mind about something I had to see it through. At that moment, we came to the ship, and that was that.

The goodbyes had to be quick, the captain said. My mother introduced herself to him and then introduced me. She told him to keep an eye on me, for I had never gone this far away from home on my own. She gave him a letter to pass on to the captain of the next ship that I would board in Barbados. They walked me to my cabin, a small space that I would share with someone else—a woman I did not know. I had never before slept in a room with someone I did not know. My father kissed me goodbye and told me to be good and to write home often. After he said this, he looked at me, then looked at the floor and swung his left foot, then looked at me again. I could see that he wanted to say something else, something that he had never said to me before, but then he just turned and walked away. My mother said, "Well," and then she threw her arms around me. Big tears streamed down her face, and it must have been that —for I could not bear to see my mother cry—which started me crying, too. She then tightened her arms around me and held me to her close, so that I felt that I couldn't breathe. With that, my tears dried up and I was suddenly on my guard. "What does she want now?" I said to myself. Still holding me close to her, she said, in a voice that raked across my skin, "It doesn't matter what you do or where you go, I'll always be your mother and this will always be your home."

I dragged myself away from her and backed off a little, and then I shook myself, as if to wake myself out of a stupor. We looked at each other for a long time with smiles on our faces, but I know the opposite of that was in my heart. As if responding to some invisible cue, we both said, at the very same moment, "Well." Then my mother turned around and walked out the cabin door. I stood there for I don't know how long, and then I remembered that it was customary to stand on deck and wave to your relatives who were returning to shore. From the deck, I could not see my father, but I could see my mother facing the ship, her eyes searching to pick me out. I removed from my bag a red cotton handkerchief that she had earlier given me for this purpose, and I waved it wildly in the air. Recognizing me immediately, she waved back just as wildly, and we continued to do this until she became just a dot in the matchbox-size launch swallowed up in the big blue sea.

I went back to my cabin and lay down on my berth. Everything trembled as if it had a spring at its very center. I could hear the small waves lap-lapping around the ship. They made an unexpected sound, as if a vessel filled with liquid had been placed on its side and now was slowly emptying out.